AF501598

Max Pemberton

A Gentleman's Gentleman

e-artnow 2021

Max Pemberton

A Gentleman's Gentleman

Mystery Novel

e-artnow, 2021
Contact: info@e-artnow.org

ISBN 978-80-273-4038-5

Contents

CHAPTER I
THE FRIENDSHIP OF LILIAN MORE

I havemet a good many in my time who professed to know a lot about Sir Nicolas Steele. I am not going to contradict them here, nor do I wish to write the life of a man whom I have served, on and off, for more years than I care to remember. If ever that's to be done, it must be the business of one who got his learning at school. All that I can speak about is that which I saw with my own eyes and heard with my own ears during the days when I was servant to him. And if my word can do any thing to set him right before the world, in so far as he can be set right, I give that word willingly, as is his due.

No man, they say, is a hero to his own valet. Maybe they speak truth, though, for my part, I wouldn't pass that for a good saying. Scandal goes as the crow flies, while a reputation for what they call virtue is often long on the road. Sometimes she never gets there at all —a trick, I fancy, she played upon Sir Nicolas Steele. The world has called him most things, from blackmailer down to thief. There aren't many mortal sins which have not been written against his name at one time or other. I alone, perhaps, know the man as he was; know his weaknesses and his strength, his good deeds and his bad. What I shall write in these papers can add nothing to the calumnies which have been put upon him by lying tongues. It is even possible that they will serve him-which is the hope of a man who has to thank him for much!

I have said that, in attempting this task, I don't mean to write a book full of all the odds and ends which those who write novels busy themselves with. My purpose is to speak of some of those curious adventures into which fortune led us together, and in which I played as much the part of a friend as of a servant. For the matter of that, I had not been a year in Sir Nicolas's service before it was plain to me that he stood in need of just that sort of help which I could give him. Daring, and nerve, and generosity, and recklessness-all these he had; but the mind to foresee, and to scheme, and to invent-that he lacked. How far I was able to make up for this, it is not for me to say; my writing must speak for itself upon that point.

When I look back upon my life during the past five years, it seems to me but a few months ago since my master was at the very ebb of his fortunes. I can recall the day as if it had been yesterday when we found ourselves in a two-pair back off Gower Street, and God alone knew where the next sovereign was to come from. We had just returned from Ireland then-it was four years ago-staggering under lies heavy enough to sink a ship. There weren't four doors in all London open to Sir Nicolas; hardly a friend who did not cross the road when we met him. Even some of those he had most right to count upon were the first to show their backs to him. As for enemies, a sum wouldn't have numbered them. You couldn't open a society paper without finding some chatter, which was like fuel to the fire of their talk. Old Lord Heresford swore he'd horsewhip him in the club; the Dublin people posted him for a swindler; there was a dozen versions of the card trouble which had driven us out of Ireland; a hundred tongues could tell you all about Margaret King, the woman who was the first to set the scandal going. Most men would have sunk under circumstances such as these; Nicky Steele did nothing of the sort. He took a two-pair back by Gower Street, and waited for a fairer wind.

"A snap of the finger for the lot of them!" said he; it was the second night we were back. "Let them bark, and be d — —d to them. Would I run away because some poor devil of a journalist is making a half a crown by me affairs? They'll shout themselves hoarse in a week, and I'll be on the road again."

"If you took my advice, sir," said I, "you'd be on the road now. You don't forget that Easter is three weeks off. There's plenty who'd be glad to see you in Paris just now."

"'Tis truth ye speak," he replied, "and if I had the money, this very night should see me moving. But what would I do in Paris with a five-pound note for my luggage? 'Tis greedy as a woman is that same city. And ten days yet to the, quarter! The devil take the luck we're having!"

"You don't hope to hear from Mr. Ames, sir?"

"'Twould be a miracle if I did, for 'tis two hundred that he owes me. Bedad, an artist who pays his debts should be put in a museum. And Jack Ames is likely to get no such distinction. But I'll be off after quarter-day, and thankful enough to shake my heels at this dirty country."

He said it all in his careless way, and he never was a man to show the white feather; but I knew that he was hit hard enough, and dreaded the days that must pass until he got his money and we were moving again. All said and done, there's no cure for a trouble of this kind like a bit of travel; and if Paris won't lift the gloom off a man's mind, he may say good-by to the doctors. I feared every hour to hear of him doing something foolish in London; and I know that he slept bad, for more than one night passed and he never got out of his arm-chair. As for the days, those he spent moping over the fire, a picture of dejection that cut your heart to see. Save one little woman-and God knows what he owed to her-there wasn't a human being in all the city who cared a button whether he was alive or dead. But Lilian More was a friend in a thousand. I believe that she saved the life of Sir Nicolas Steele.

He had met her some years before, I don't exactly know where; and it happened that they ran against each other at the corner of Oxford Street on the night after he had spoken to me about going away. She was a slim little thing, not one you would have picked out on a stage as a beauty, but a wonderful woman for kindness, and just as sweet-tempered as any creature I ever clapped eyes on. When she came into a house it was like opening the front door to a breeze of laughter. She had a bright word and a smile for every one, just the prettiest possible smile you could see; and this was the more surprising since her face was the face of a woman who had suffered much and was suffering still. I remember once going into our little parlor, where she had been taking tea with Sir Nicolas, and finding her sitting over the fire with her head resting in her hands; and when I lighted the gas quickly, and she looked up, there were tears in her eyes. My master had gone into the other room to write a letter at the moment; and, of course, I pretended to see nothing. When he came back in a few minutes' time, the whole place was rippling with her laughter. For that was the way of her,—then and always, I don't doubt,—high spirits for others, and misery for herself. How many women must play a part like that!

Nicky met her just when he was most in want of a cheering word. He had not been out of the house for three days, and when he did go out it was only as far as Oxford Street to buy one of the papers which was telling some new story about him. Directly he got back I knew that something had happened. He was a different man from what he had been twenty minutes before, and the lines in his face seemed almost to have been wiped out by his walk.

"Hildebrand," he cried, pretty well before he was in the house, "ye'll lay out my clothes, please; I'm going to the theatre."

"To the theatre, sir?" exclaimed I, just as astonished as a man could be.

"'Tis so," he went on; "and I'll be supping away after. Ye may set out the glasses, and go to bed when you please. Do you remember me speaking of little Lilian More, that I used to know in Birmingham? Well, she's playing at the Royalty, and she's asked me down. I'm to sup with her and her one-armed brother-in-law at Chelsea. Sure, 'tis as good as quinine to hear her laugh, any day."

I said nothing in answer to this, though I was very glad to think that he had met some one who would take his mind off the trouble. Though I did not know Lilian More then, I began to hope he was not going to make a fool of himself, for he put on his dress-clothes anyhow, and such was not his way when he had the mind to please a woman, he being extraordinary vain, as some of my stories will tell. I knew well enough that an hour wouldn't have served him at the glass if the lady had been any thing but a friend to him-and friend he regarded her right through to the end. What it was on her side is not for me to speak about. I believe that she loved him,—I shall believe that to my dying day,—and for love of him she paid with her life, as my story will show.

Well, he went to the theatre, and next day he got up at twelve, and was as busy as a man could be. Almost his first words were talk about Miss More, and that he kept up all the time I was shaving him.

"She has the spirits of twenty," he said; "there was never a brighter little woman born. 'Twas good luck that sent me to Oxford Street for sure! Ye'll see Mrs. Leverty about the lunch I spoke of, though I doubt she'll do much."

"You didn't mention no lunch to me, sir," said I while I helped him into his best frock-coat. "Are you looking for any company?"

"Indeed, and I am; there's Miss More coming, and her brother-in-law, Mr. Connoley-him that has one arm. A strange man he is, too, as full of tales as a bowl of good punch of whiskey. Ye must just talk sweetly to the old lady down stairs, and see what ye can do. 'Tis not much I have at the moment, but I'll not forget her when quarter-day is here."

"We've told her that pretty often already, sir," said I. "If she gets what I've promised her, Mrs. Leverty will be a rich woman on quarter-day."

"Be hanged to that!" cried he. "Ye've a sweet way with you, and will persuade her. 'Twould never do to sit down to bread and cheese and kisses. Have I any cigarettes in the house?"

"You smoked the last in bed this morning," said I; "but we've credit at the tobacconist's, and that will be all right. Perhaps I can manage a couple of bottles of champagne from Williams. I'll tell him you've good company, and that we will recommend him. It's astonishing how many wine merchants live on recommendations, sir. One chap who can't pay recommends another who don't mean to pay, and so they keep the ball rolling. It's a beautiful trade, but I've no fancy for it myself."

He laughed at this, and I went off to get his lunch ready. It was hard work to talk over the old woman who let us the lodgings, but I made a bit of love to her, and when she was smoothed down, I got the champagne from Williams. By the time I was back again Miss More and her brother-in-law were in the sitting-room, and she was already busy putting his ornaments straight and arranging a few flowers she had brought him. It was astonishing to see how her laughing little face brightened up that dingy old apartment. She was here, there, and everywhere, like a butterfly in a garden, and I don't believe she stopped talking from the minute she entered the door until the hansom took her away again.

"Pat," I heard her say-all the women called him Pat—"what a place to get into, Pat! Do you know I've a good mind to ask you where you keep the pig?"

"And wouldn't I be glad to tell you that he was under the table," said he; "'tis not me that has the money to think of pigs just now. Bedad, it's myself I'll be taking to market if times don't change. Will ye be smoking, Mr. Connoley? We've tobacco still in the ship, and that's something."

Connoley, you must know, was the queerest fish I've ever seen out of Billingsgate. He was a long, lean man, with his left hand cut off at the wrist, and his face tattooed by the roots of his beard until it looked like the chest of a sailor. Many's the queer tale he has told me in his time. To listen to him, you would think that no such fire-eating devil ever came out of Texas. Yet I discovered afterward that he was only a barrister on half-pay, so to speak, and that he had a wife and ten children in a little slum off Sloane Street. What work he did, or in whose service he did it, the Lord only knows. I never saw him, so far as my recollection goes, busy with any thing but a pipe—a great German pipe with a cherry stem, which he carried everywhere, like other men carry a stick. An odder figure than his you would never see. The first thing he did when he came to our rooms was to change his boots for a pair of carpet-slippers. Then he stuck himself in an arm-chair by the fire, and I don't think he opened his lips for an hour and a half. Food made no difference to him. He would take a fork in his left hand, and a pipe in his right. When he did speak, it was to tell you how he killed three Bulgarians in Sofia, and had a mysterious fortune awaiting him in the East. He promised to take me there when the time was right, and I couldn't answer him for laughing.

But all this is outside my story. What I wanted to write down is that Connoley smoked, and Nicky Steele laughed, and Miss More told stories all the time our little luncheon party was on. When it was done, they went off together to the West End, and I saw nothing of my master until. one o'clock in the morning. He was lively enough then, and all his depression and melancholy seemed troubles of a year rather than that of twenty-four hours ago.

"Bedad," said he, as I mixed him a whiskey and soda and gave him his smoking-coat, "'tis the best little woman in London, she is, and the merriest. I haven't stopped laughing since I left the house; yet what I laughed at, God only knows. That's the way of a witty woman. Her laugh is like the song of a bird in spring. You don't ask why the bird sings, but you tune yourself up to the chorus. I'll forget that I was ever in Ireland if I am with her long."

"Is she living in London now, sir?" I asked.

"Indeed and she is, though 'tis a poor place of a cabin that she has. I'm to lunch there to-morrow at two. Ye'll not let me forget that-two o'clock sharp, and to the play afterward, if I can manage it — —"

"You're not likely to have any engagement," said I.

"Ye speak truth," he replied; "but the money it is that makes a free man. Maybe Jack Ames will pay me this week. I wish I could think so."

"Maybe we shall see a comet in the sky, sir," was my answer; and with that I took myself off to bed.

CHAPTER II
A HOUSE OF GLOOM IN CHELSEA

During the next ten days it seemed to me that I did little but run backward and forward between Gower Street and Trafalgar Square, at Chelsea, where Miss More had her flat, A queer place it was too-just a bit of a studio, one of six, all built up a yard, which might have belonged to a stable; and as bare as a barn save for the merry little woman who lived in it. A right pleasant welcome she always gave me, I must say, and many's the glass of good Scotch whiskey I have drank in her parlor.

"We must do our best for your master," she would say while she took out her purse-and that she did every time I went to her rooms; "we must do our best for him, and see that he is not left too much alone. I know what it is to want friends myself. Things will come all right presently, and he will forget that this has happened. You must make it your business to see that he does not mope in the house. Encourage him to go out, and get him away to Paris as soon as possible-you understand what I mean?"

"I understand, miss," said I; "and thank you kindly for thinking of it. I wish it was all as nice and straight as your words. But how a man who hasn't five pounds to his back is to cross the Channel, I really don't know. He isn't no Captain Webb, miss; and I don't forget that we're in the middle of March."

She laughed at this, but she was never one to laugh long when I was alone with her; and presently she became very serious.

"He did not tell me it was as bad as that," she said-and I could see that she was thinking hard—"but now I understand many things. We must find a way out of this, Hildebrand. I am sure we can do it between us. You won't forget the letter, and be sure that he comes to the theatre to-night. When one wants to cry, there is no place like a gloomy house to cry in."

"That's true, miss," I replied; "though, if you ask me, all the crying in Europe won't make a five-pound note of a tailor's bill when your credit has gone walking. I was never one to believe in the waterworks myself, nor is Sir Nicolas, I make sure. A wonderful light heart he has most times, though I must say that I never remember such a three months as this year has brought him. If it hadn't been for you, God knows what would have happened to him."

"Oh, I have done nothing," she answered—"nothing at all; any friend would have done as much. I cannot forget what I owed to him in Birmingham five years ago. He was very good to me then, and I should be ashamed not to try and help him here."

Now, this was news to me, for I knew nothing at that time of any past relations between Sir Nicolas and herself, though I could quite imagine that any man would have gone out of his way to do a turn to so kind-hearted a creature. Yet what kindness he had shown to her, or in what position they had stood to each other, I knew no more than the dead. Her whole life seemed to me to be as great a mystery as any thing I had ever heard of. She had plenty of money, and yet she lived in a hovel where I wouldn't have stabled a donkey. She had the grace and fascination of twenty women, and yet there was not a whisper of a love affair in her life. They told you at the theatre of a hundred offers of marriage which she had declined; they spoke of the "opportunities" she had given the cold shoulder to; of the extraordinary silence which she maintained whenever her own life was mentioned. No nun in a convent could have blotted out her past more successfully. People declared that they worshipped her. They could say no more; and even the boldest of them never dared to put a second embarrassing question to the woman who knew so well how to keep her own secrets and to defend them.

I thought of all these things on my way from Chelsea to Gower Street, and while I could make nothing of them, I was far from easy about our own future. A big-hearted man like Nicky Steele, who never said no to a woman in his life, was always dangerous when there was a woman hanging about him; and I knew well enough that little Lilian More worshipped the ground he trod on. It did not suit my plan at all that he should wind up by marrying a bit of a play-actress; for I felt his title would be worth money abroad, and abroad I meant that he should go. None the less was I sure that there was danger in the situation, and with that danger I determined to cope.

I saw this just when I arrived at our own place, expecting to find my master impatient for his lunch. I found him engaged with something much more important. He had a scrap of a letter in his hand when I came in; and he was walking up and down the parlor, still wearing his dressing-gown, but looking for all the world like a man who has been scared half out of his wits. Nor did he let any time pass before he told me what the matter was.

"Read this," said he, holding out the dirty, crumpled sheet of note; "read it, and tell me if you ever saw the like to it?"

I took the letter and found that it contained two lines of crabbed and winding writing, done in pencil. It was some minutes before I could make head or tail of the thing; but when at last I read it, I was just as much astonished as he was.

"If you are seen at Lilian More's again, I will blow your brains out."

This was all of it-no address, no date, no signature; note-paper which you might have bought at a farthing the sheet, and a handwriting which might have been a parson's, and might have been a schoolboy's. And as if to blind us further, the postmark was Chancery Lane, which, as all the world knows, has nothing particular to do with Chelsea.

"Well," said Sir Nicolas, while I stood gaping at the letter like a board-school boy might gape at a slice of Greek, "can ye read it?"

"Oh, I can read it all right, sir," I replied; "it ain't a difficult handwriting to read."

"Indeed, and it is not. I call it altogether a very pretty production; 'tis worthy of the murdering scoundrel who had the impudence to send it."

"Then you know who sent it, sir?"

"Should I know who sent it? The devil take me if I have the ghost of an idea, unless it's the barrister with the one arm. 'Tis a queer letter entirely."

"That's true, sir; but I don't think Mr. Connoley wrote it. If he was having a bit of fun with you, he'd set about it different to that. You don't forget his three Bulgarians and his fortune in the East? What's more, he likes to see you at Chelsea. I'm as sure of that as of my own name."

"Then who the blazes would send such a thing?"

"That I can't say off-hand. Maybe one of the young men who hang about Miss More at the theatre. It isn't to be expected that all of them would see her come here and say nothing about it. You don't know of any friends that would have the right to speak for her, sir?"

"Not the shadow of one. When I met her in Birmingham eight years ago, her father was living—a bookseller down at Oxford he was; but he died three years ago, and I never heard that she had a brother."

"Then it's one of her theatre friends," said I, "and, if he comes my way, I'll wipe him down with a hickory towel. Don't you trouble about that, sir. A young man in' love is fond of flying to pistols-when he don't fly to whiskey and soda. You toss the thing into the fire, and I'll do the rest."

He heard me out, and then he seemed persuaded.

"Bedad," said he, "I believe ye're right, and it's some jealous little boy out of the wings that is anxious to crow upon my own dung-heap. The impudence of the devil! 'Tis as good as a play that any one should think I would be marrying Miss More. They'll laugh finely at the theatre when I pass it round."

"I wouldn't do that for a bit, sir," said I; "we may as well try and find out how the land lies. There are plenty of lunatics walking about the world, and it's just as well to know what road they take — —"

"Would ye have me seek police protection, then? 'Tis funny I would look with a policeman at my heels for the matter of a penny letter from a maniac. Faith, I'll just put it in my pocket-book, and show it to Miss More when she comes. 'Twill be a good laugh for the pair of us."

He seemed pleased with this idea, and, sure enough, when she came up with Connoley in the afternoon, the three of them had a rare laugh over it.

"'Tis to many we are, Lilian," said my master, reading the letter out aloud, while the one-armed barrister smoked harder than ever—"to marry we are, and here is the man who will forbid the banns, d'ye see? The murdering scoundrel, to want to blow me brains out!"

"He'll never do that, Nicky," said Connoley; "that's beyond him. He may excavate the cavity, but as for blowing your brains out, why, ye can't blow out what isn't there to blow. Now, when I was in Bulgaria-you remember the three men I shot there — —"

"Be hanged to your three men!" cried Sir Nicolas. "Is it not yerself that has shot them twenty times in this very room?"

"And why not?" says Connoley. "If there's a more curious story than mine since I met 'The Raven' in the Strand, I'd be glad to hear of it. But ye've no literary faculty, Nicky-not a trace of it."

"There was nothing so vulgar ever run in me family," exclaimed my master. "We never came lower than pathriots since I can remember. Ye'll not claim to be a cousin of mine, Roderick. Bedad, I'll change my name if you do. 'Tis a sweet name is More, and I would carry it finely."

He looked at Miss More when he said this, and all three of them laughed together.

"You seem to think it a very good joke, Pat," said she.

"I have heard no better since I came out of Ireland!" cried he. "That they should want to blow out my brains! I knew it would amuse you finely."

With this laugh they changed the subject; but during the afternoon I saw Miss More with tears in her eyes, as I have told you, and I am sure it was a very poor joke to her, though Nicky was blind to the end of it, and never so much as suspected what I knew all along. As for the silly letter, he forgot that as soon as he had torn it up. I heard him making an appointment to go down to Chelsea that very night, and get a picture of Lilian More in her theatre clothes. He was always messing about with photographs and stinking chemicals, and if he took one picture of that bright little woman, he took fifty. I have one now stuck on the mantle-shelf of my room here—I burned a dozen before he went down to Derbyshire and nearly married Miss Oakley there; but the photograph of Miss More in her theatre clothes is in the hands of the man who, in some sort of way, has the best right to it, though God help him when he looks at it, say I.

CHAPTER III
THE MESSAGE

The arrangement was that Sir Nicolas should go down and take the picture at half-past eleven that night.

"I'll take ye by the magnesium light, Lilian," said he; "and after that we'll go and get supper somewhere. 'Tis a beautiful light, if ye know how to handle it. Ye won't forget to put on the bull's eyes and the crown."

"Why not take Roderick, too, and call it 'Beauty and the Beast'?" said she.

"'T would be a libel on my race," said he; and with that they parted, she going to the theatre, while he went to get a bit of dinner in Old Compton Street.

Half-past ten had struck when he came back again. It never occurred to me that he would want my company, but such proved the case.

"Ye may help me to carry the camera," said he, while he began to get the dry plates ready; "and, if ye're not very tired, I'd be glad to take you as far as Miss More's place. 'Tis not afraid I am of a paltry threatening letter, but we couldn't do with a scene just now, and there's plenty of fools ready to make one when they're a bit spoony over a woman. I won't keep you the half of an hour."

I was a little surprised at this, for he seemed to have forgotten all about the letter; but I went ready enough, and, what's more, I took a good thick stick in my hand when I started.

"If there is any puppy who desires particular to bark, I'm his man," said I to myself as I got in the cab. I knew well enough that *he* was right when he said that we could not afford to have a scene. There was too much talked of already for us to be advertising ourselves on the newspaper bills. And that I meant to prevent, all the puppies in London notwithstanding.

We were half an hour, I suppose, driving from Gower Street to Chelsea. It was near about a quarter to twelve when we arrived at Miss More's studio; but even then we seemed to have come too early. Her flat, as I have told you, was one of six, built up an entry. A housekeeper opened the outer gate, and, once inside the long passage, you saw six little front doors all standing in a row, like so many green shutters. Miss More's door was the last of these, and when we came up to it we found it locked.

"She'll be still at the theatre," said the old woman who showed us in. "'Tain't often as this 'ouse sees her before midnight, that I do know. I'll let you in, and you can bide till she comes."

She opened the door with a key she carried at her waist, and we went into the studio, which was as dark as a prison and cold as a ship's deck on a winter's night. I judged by the feel of it that the place had not seen a fire since morning, and a curtain drawn over the glass window in the roof kept out the light like a shutter might have done. It was a room which did not strike comfort into you at the best of times; but a more cheerless apartment at such a time of night I never want to enter. I was shivering like a boy in a swimming-bath two minutes after the door closed upon us, and I don't believe Nicky was any better.

"The blazes of a place it is, for sure," said he. "To think that she lives alone in such a hovel as this. It can't be for want of the money; they say she's earning twenty pounds a week, and will earn more. Strike a light, will ye? I'd be more at home in a vault, I take leave to think."

"I'll have a light quick enough, sir," said I, "once I've got this camera down. Mind how you tread. There's a cushion here, or something—I feel it under my foot-and this is a couch, I suppose."

I had stumbled against something while I spoke to him, and when I put out my hand to see what it was, I had the greatest start that ever I can remember.

"Good God, sir," said I, the sweat starting sudden to my forehead, "there's some one lying on this sofa!"

"You don't mean that!" cried he.

"As I'm a living man, I do. Hold the camera a minute, and let me see."

He took the camera out of my hands, and I struck a lucifer. Its poor passing light lit up our corner of the room maybe for ten seconds before we were in the dark again. But the sight which we both saw is one which I shall never forget to my dying day. Miss More herself lay huddled up on the sofa, her left hand touching the floor, her right hand supporting her head. Her face was the face of one sleeping restfully, yet so pale and unearthly looking that I knew she was dead. And in death all the kindness and sweetness of her nature seemed written ten times over upon her placid features. It might have been a child lying there —a child that had died laughing into a mother's eyes.

For some seconds neither of us spoke. I never remember a minute like that when we stood dumb and trembling in the face of death, and the dark seemed to hide the whole of the awful truth from us. When at last my master opened his lips, his voice was like a whisper of a man in a vault.

"Run for help and a doctor," said he. "God grant we are dreaming!"

He staggered out with me to the door, and our cries brought the old hag from the porter's lodge. She had a lantern in her hand, and she and my master went back to the studio together. When I returned in ten minutes' time —a doctor at my heels —I found the two together chafing the dead woman's hands, and trying to force brandy between her lips. Nor do I know which was the whiter of the two-my master or the dead girl who had befriended him.

"Oh, for God's sake do something, doctor!" said he. "'Tis the sweetest creature in the world to die like this! Ye'll not tell me that there's no hope!"

But the doctor said nothing. He was listening for a beat of the heart —a thing I was sure he would never hear. Five minutes, perhaps, he bent over the little figure of the woman whose laughter had been music to every soul she knew. Then he rose like a man who has done all possible.

"I come too late," he said; "your friend is dead from laudanum poisoning."

A quick glance round the room gave strength to his words. There was a blue bottle upon the table, and a letter by it. The doctor picked up the bottle and smelt it; Sir Nicholas took the letter and read it.

> "Pat (it said), take my picture for the love of auld lang syne; take it as I lie when you will see me, and send it to the man whose address is here. I can do no more for him. God bless all who have done me any kindness!"

My master shuddered.

"God forgive any one that ever did harm to so sweet a woman," said he.

CHAPTER IV
OUT OF THE NIGHT

There was no sleep for either of us that night; nor, I think, did Sir Nicolas take off his clothes for two days after Miss More died. The black mystery of the whole thing, the extraordinary surprise of it, was more than he or I could cope with. We had seen the dead woman in the afternoon as merry and as light-hearted as a child; she had asked us to come down to her rooms and to take her picture just as one might ask a friend to pay a pleasant call. What had happened in the between time, what trouble or disappointment or sorrow had come upon her, I knew no more than the dead. That she loved Sir Nicolas Steele I was sure; that her death was in some way to be connected with the strange letter of warning my master had received was equally obvious. But who the writer of that letter was, and what was his claim upon Lilian More, I had yet to find out.

I say that I had yet to find out, and this is true. A jury returned a plain verdict, —a merciful verdict, you may be sure, —and the police, who had taken charge of the writing we found in the room, could add no information to our own. They went to the house to which we had been asked to send the photograph, and found it in a slum in Hammersmith-an empty house, once kept by a woman who let lodgings, but then deserted and almost in ruins. Nor was there any friend of Miss More who could add to what we knew. As for Connoley, he had gone to Scotland the very day his sister-in-law died. No one knew his address, and we took it that he saw nothing in the papers. Indeed, he told me, when I met him in Paris a year later, that he never learned the news until a month after his kinswoman was dead.

All this did not help me in getting at what I wanted; nor was my master any readier in doing what I could not do.

"'Tis a story of trouble, ye may be sure," he said to me on the second morning, "but I doubt if any man will write it. Whatever it was, it must have happened after I gave her the promise to take her picture. 'Twould be terrible to think that she meant it otherwise."

"That's so, sir," said I. "Yet, when a woman is driven to that state, God knows what she won't think of! Be sure of this, that she wanted somebody to know she was dead, and this was the queer idea she had of telling him."

"Would it be the man who wrote me the murdering letter?" he asked.

"I have no doubt of it-her husband, very likely, if she had one. At least, that's what appears on the face of it."

"I never thought of that," he said quickly. "It may be as you say, but he'll go wanting the picture, any way. I wouldn't have taken it for a thousand down."

"There you're wrong, sir," said I; "if we're prudent men we'll find out who this person is, and what he has against us. And the picture may help us. It's here, in my pocket, any way."

I never saw a man more astonished.

"Ye had it taken, then?" he cried.

"That's so, sir. I called in a photographer yesterday, and here's the print."

He took the picture and looked at for a long time.

"Well," said he, "we must all come to that, some day or other. Good God! it makes me cold to think of it. And the sweetest little woman that ever drew breath. Ye won't leave it about the place? I couldn't sleep with a thing like that in my rooms."

I told him that I would not, and I put the picture away. It was clear that I could do nothing with it until he should give me some information which I did not then possess; and, as it turned out, I had almost forgotten the affair when that information came to me. Indeed, three weeks had passed and Jack Ames had paid the two hundred, and we were on the eve of going up to Yorkshire, when, just as Nicky had left Gower Street one night to dine at the Green House Club, there came a ring at our bell and a tall man stepped into the hall and asked for him. There was only a bit of a gas-flare burning in the passage then, and the man being in the shadow, I couldn't very well see his face; but I noticed that his clothes were very shabby and that he wore a rough overcoat which was a size too small for him. And his hat was an old silk one; but so black inside that a regiment of heads might have worn it.

"You desire to see Sir Nicolas Steele?" said I, not much liking the look of him, for he stood there just like a mute.

"I want to see him," he answered in a thick, husky voice, "and to see him at once."

"Well," said I, not liking his manner, "I've a notion that you can't do that, since he isn't in the house."

"Not in the house!" cried he, losing his temper all in a minute. "Oh! I'll soon know about that. Come, no lies-where is he, and where is the other?"

With this word, he took a step forward into the passage, and I saw his face for the first time. It was the face of an exceedingly handsome man, but there was a queer look in the eyes, such as I have never seen in the eyes of a human being before or since. Try as I might I couldn't describe that strange expression of his. Anger, determination, cruelty, all these were in it, but there was something beyond, a look as though the man had no power to keep his thoughts on any one thing for two minutes together; not the peering gaze of the madman, but the glance of one weakened by long illness until the nerves were shattered and the brain unhinged.

"Where is your master?" he repeated, forcing his way up the hall. "I mean to speak to him."

"Then you'll have to come to-morrow," said I. "You don't suppose I'm going to work a miracle for your particular benefit! I tell you that he isn't in the house'"

"Oh!" said he, drawing back and seeming to think of it. "Do you know if he has gone to Chelsea?"

"To Chelsea?" cried I, though his words sent me cold all over. "What would he do at Chelsea?"

"He would be with Mrs. Hadley," said he, though I could see that his mind did not follow his words.

"That's a name I never heard before, so I really can't say," I replied.

"You know her as Lilian More," he exclaimed, turning his eyes upon me quickly. "He is with her now! Don't tell me lies, or I will serve you as I mean to serve him!"

"Sir!" said I quickly, for his words shocked me, "Miss More died three weeks ago."

Now at this he did not break out or make any scene, as I thought he would do. It was wonderful to watch the manner of him; his brain seeming to grasp the truth for a minute, only to let it go in the next. As for his eyes, they were never still, and his look passed unceasingly from one object to the other.

"Three weeks ago," he said, just like a man dreaming, while he took up his hat mechanically. "That could not be; I was with her then."

"Then you are a relation?" said I.

"I am her husband," he replied; and the remembrance of that fact caused him to hold himself erect and to look me straight in the face. "I am her husband, and if any thing like that had happened, should not I be the first to know of it?"

"Properly you ought to be, sir," said I, "but perhaps you weren't in London then."

"I have been in London for three months," he answered, raising his voice suddenly. "I know you are telling me a lie-by God! how dare you?"

"It is no lie," I replied; and sorry for him I was, for the tears were now running down his face like rain. "If you are the lady's husband, sir, it is you who ought to have the picture I have been carrying about with me since the day after Miss More died. I'll fetch it for you."

With this I ran upstairs to my room and took the photograph out of my box. I was away a couple of minutes, perhaps; but when I came down again he was still standing fingering his hat in the hall, and he didn't appear to have moved a foot since I left him. I was half frightened to give him the picture, so strange was his manner; but the dead woman had wished it, and I meant to respect her words.

"Here it is, sir," said I. "It was her wish that you should have it, and no thought of ours."

He made no answer, but snatched the frame out of my hand. His restless eyes seemed to fall upon the portrait for a minute, then to rest upon the floor, and after that again upon me! It was plain that his dazed brain was only beginning to find the truth.

"She was my wife," he said very slowly, after a long pause. "Oh, God, help me! I shall never hold her in my arms again."

He saw this, and thrusting the picture into his breast, he turned to leave the house.

"Shall I give my master any message, sir?" I asked.

"Tell him that I came here to strike him dead," said he; and, before I could answer, he had disappeared down the street.

It was the first and last time I ever saw Robert Hadley-for that was his full name; but ten days later he wrote a letter from Charing Cross Hospital to Sir Nicolas, and begged my master to go and see him. And this was the way his story came to us, and with it the story of Lilian More.

She had married him in Birmingham, a year after Sir Nicolas met her there. He was a well-to-do widower then, with one little child—a girl three years old; but six months after his marriage he began to nip with his business acquaintances, and in a year he was a confirmed dipsomaniac. Business, friends, wife, and child-all these became nothing to him. He went down the ladder of self-respect fast, until he had no longer a home, and his wife was driven to get what sort of a living she could as a play-actress. That he made her life a hell to her I have no sort of doubt; but while the child lived, the woman was content to work and to slave for love of it. What she put up with from the man's temper and brutality and jealousies God only knows; for his affection for her was strong to the last, and I believe he would have shot any man who spoke twice to her. At the time we first met her in London he was in a private hospital; but the child was dead-killed by a blow of his, as more than one whisperer says, though God forbid that I should charge him with it. Be that as it may, the little one's death robbed Lilian More of all she cared to live for; and the end was what I have told.

But of all the women I ever met, she was the sweetest and the truest-and that I will say with my last breath.

CHAPTER V
THE JUSTIFICATION OF RODERICK CONNOLEY

It is my business in these memoirs to speak chiefly of the many strange things which happened to Sir Nicolas Steele during the last three or four years I served him; but I do not know why that should prevent me saying a last word here about Roderick Connoley, the barrister, and the many queer stories he told us during our stay in London and afterward in Paris. How far he believed these stories, what foundation in fact they had, it is not for me to decide. That he had lived a curious life, I knew well; that he had lost his left hand in his boyhood was a truth which my eyes told me unmistakably. But how he came to lose it, if his own account is not to be believed, is a thing I am not competent to speak about.

It was a year after the death of Lilian More that we met this remarkable man again; and then we ran against him quite by accident in Paris, where we had been living some months, and allowing London to forget that we existed. He came almost every day to the Hôtel de Lille, where we were stopping; and it was there that he gave my master the manuscript of the following story, which contains his own account of his deformity. Sir Nicolas declared at that time that he would send the writing to one of the London papers; but he never did so, and when I left him in Russia last year, I took the pages with me to America. In this way I am able to give the tale without altering a line or a word that Roderick Connoley wrote, and, for my part, I say this-that a stranger tale of an accident I never read.

THE SEVEN MEN WITH THE SEVEN HANDS, AND THE STRANGE ADVENTURES OF A BARRISTER

Part I—The Raven

The rain was pitiless, and the night was dark. There was pretence of light from the floors of the restaurant and the misted street lamps, but none of it came upon the slum where the stage-door opened. For the fiftieth time, as the clock struck eleven, I drew my cape around me, and cursed the folly which led me to pace a stone-yard and ape the idiocy of boyhood when maturer years had come. And "The Raven" did the same, I doubt not.

I had watched "The Raven" many a night as I had kept a vigil akin to this. For whom did he wait, and why was he here? Had he done as I had done-thrown sense to the winds for a chit in lace petticoats; staked all on a baby-face which smiled upon him in the second row of the stalls, but smiled not in the dark of the exit hour? I judged so, for no man would keep such a watch at such an hour if madness did not lead him. The thought begot my sympathy for him. I had seen his face on other nights, and knew that he could hope for nothing, for his was the face of a wizened old man, long-drawn in solitude and bitterness; and the black locks which fell upon his shoulders seemed a mockery of time. I called him "The Raven," and for many nights we watched each other as beasts that would quarrel, but lack the courage. He knew my secret, I did not doubt; for it was a tale in all the theatre that I had waited for Lelia Winnie since the autumn had gone, and that I had spoken no word to her. There were others-richer, perhaps-of great name, and able to move managers. I had not the password; none showed me deference; and Lelia danced on, a stranger to me.

The rain was pitiless, and the night was dark. But Lelia did not pass out when the others left. I had taken up a position close to the stage-door, and scanned the faces of those going into the night, but hers was not among them. Bright faces they were for the most part-the faces of girls moved by all the curious romance of the theatre, moved to desire of excitement, in some cases to desire of shame; a merry throng of irresponsibles, who would die peeresses or paupers, in old family mansions or in the gutter. And they went to lovers and to suppers with the gas-jets lighting up their faces, and the black still thick upon their eyes, while I waited as the rain fell and struck me, cold and chill, with disappointment. I had forgotten "The Raven" as the crowd surged out; but he, too, was looking, and when all had gone he spoke to me with a voice hard as the crack of dry wood:

"Again!"

It was the one word only, but I turned upon him with a sharp reply, when I saw, by the light streaming through the still open door, that there was a smile upon his lips, while he gripped my arm tightly with his hand.

"Again, and unto seventy times! Seek and find-seek and find-like all the fools before and since, unto seventy times!"

He was either a madman or a fanatic, and I determined to let him be, giving him smile for smile and jest for jest; but he gripped my arm yet tighter, saying:

"Come!"

I went with him down the passage and into the open Strand, passing from the valley of the disreputable to the highway of the respectable going home to supper and to bed. Nor did he pause until we had gone westward many paces, when he drew me with him to a small eating-house by Covent Garden, and there we sat. In the clearer light of the room I had that opportunity to observe him which the dark of the passage had denied me; and in truth he was a strange man, much furrowed in the flesh, and glittering with the light of madness in his eyes. But he drank full well from the cup set before him, and there were diamonds, large and lustrous, upon the fingers which he raised. I waited for him to speak, for the advance had been of his, and not of my seeking; but he drank many glasses before he spoke, and then it was in the tone of the hard-mouthed cynic who has bitten into life and found gall for his palate.

"Again, Roderick Connoley"—having my name in what way I knew not—"again, and the woman is no nearer-no nearer, but more distant, while you wait."

"What my business is to you, I cannot think," I answered, "or why you should seek to discuss it."

He replied with a loud guffaw, throwing his sod- den cape over his shoulders so that the rain ran down upon his shirt and over the heavy-linked chain hanging at his waistcoat.

"Why should I discuss it?" he said. "Because, my friend, the only serious thing that man does discuss is woman. Since the world began he has discussed her; since the day that there was chaos and she sat a star in the heavens; and he will discuss her when the world is no more. Sometimes it will be the good thought from which springs the tree of life; sometimes it will be with the more base and degrading idea of self, which they call possession-such an idea as moves you now, the evil, ill-gotten desire for a woman who may be innocent, but whom you would make guilty before the day comes-you, I say, who find life at a stage-door!"

He pointed threateningly with his finger across the table, and I knew that he spoke the truth. I could find no answer to his accusation, so I drank deeply of the wine and avoided the search of his eyes. But I continued to feel his look; almost the terrible grasp of his hand upon mine. There was silence for some minutes before he spoke again, and then it was with another voice, as though one had put ice upon his tongue.

"One fool often makes two," he said, as he called for a second bottle of wine. " Forget that I have spoken, for I am but the servant of the Master, and how shall the servant speak when the Master has not spoken? I brought you here for your ends, not for mine, and therefore would serve your ends before my own. You are Roderick Connoley, a barrister, with little money and with less employment; your life, for what it is worth, is a dream mostly dreamed in tobacco-smoke; and what you lack in performance at the moment you find in promise for the future. As a so-called man about town, you are condescending enough to patronize the vices, for which you care little, but in the true pleasures of living you remain a child. In this respect you are as other men, for how many of the thousands who drift on the sea of enjoyment in this city know any thing of those treasures which Life can give to him who understands her? I have watched you as I have watched others, and have been moved to pity for you. I have even spoken to the Master, who has listened to me as I have talked of yon, and has made known his will about you. This night your lesson in pleasure shall begin; but it remains with you to profit all or to lose all. At this moment I say no more, for the hour is at hand, and we go. Look! the clock is about to strike midnight."

He rose up from the table, this amiable madman I had met, and I knew not how to humor him. I remembered that it was a terrible night, the rain falling pitilessly, and the streets empty; so I followed the old man into the street, and entered the single brougham that was at the curbstone. It was an adventure, and why should I not pursue it?

Part II-The Lord of the Hundred Lanterns

When we left Coven t Garden we seemed to drive by way of Bloomsbury toward the north of London. The rain was still falling, but the clouds skirmished over the heavens, leaving gaps through which the stars shone, and there was light from the moon newly risen above the endless roofing. I had a mind to ask my companion whither he went; but he appeared to be sleeping as he reclined deeply in the cushions, and I, in my turn, was almost overpowered by an incontrollable drowsiness. It was just at the moment when I opened my eyes for the last time-eyes then almost fixed in sleep-that I observed a strange movement on the old man's part; for he started up of a sudden, holding something to my nostrils, and in that moment I fell asleep.

The sensations of waking have been described often. I shall not attempt to describe them again, saying only that, when I awoke from that which appeared to me an unusually long sleep, it was with the sense of a profound delight and realization of ease. I seemed to be sunken deeply in a bed of silk, whereof the huge cushions towered up around me, so that, as my eyes opened, I saw nothing but the roof of the room in which I lay. Gilded spandrels richly dowered with mosaic united in a star of silver in the centre of the chamber, and from the silver star shot down a soft white light that drew the eyes in sympathy and yet bathed them in content. There was something so rich, so resplendent in all this maze of gold-work, in the flow of the steady rays of white light that poured upon me, in the ease of the bed whereon I rested, that I lay for many minutes content to let the mystery be. What did it matter? I suffered from some dream; such things as men shape in that keen moment of imagination when the brain wakes and the body is yet sleeping; but I would not be fooled by them.

I thought thus, and closed my eyes, opening them again when some minutes had gone. The light was still shining, and it shone with a greater power, as it seemed to me, making clear the darker portions of the room, lighting the niches and the black recesses. The air I breathed seemed laden with a strange perfume, as of the perfume of unknown flowers; but to breathe it was to take strength, to feel a newer energy and a newer life. I looked around the chamber, raising myself upon my elbows in the great bed, and sitting up so that I saw all the wondrous sight. It was a great room, banked up by twenty couches,—for that upon which I rested proved to be a couch,—and, as I judged, at least a hundred silver lanterns hung down from its painted roof. All the upper portions-the metopes in the frieze of the entablature, and the frieze itself-were covered with strange Eastern pictures depicting fables and tales from the myths of Greece and the richer stories of the East. But no pen may tell of the splendor of the mosaics let into the painted walls, or of the paintings which filled the lower panels. When I looked at length from the walls to the centre of the room the sight that met my gaze was not less bewildering. There were vases of jasper and of agate, from which there stood out wide-spreading palms and the lesser palms of the forests of the East; there were tables studded with gems and with precious stones, the like of which I had seen in no land; there were hookahs in pure amber, and smaller lamps in amethyst stone from which the vapor rose. Many smaller tables placed by the couches were heaped up with fruit such as was not then to be had in London, and there were goblets chased after the fashion of the chalice known to the Western Church. I saw that a dish of the fruit and one of these goblets had been placed at the foot of my own bed, and I drank of the wine,—a deep draught and luscious,—and as I drank the sensation of pleasure, pure and without blemish, came upon me. Perhaps for the first time in my life I lived-lived in an existence which no tongue can make clear; an existence which promised to be infinite, unmarred by any bridge of death, wanting nothing of the promise of priests; an existence of the imagination, in which the body had no part. And in the very ecstasy of living I leaned back in my cushions and closed my eyes to dream.

When I opened them again it was to look into the face of an old man. He sat squat upon his haunches, with the mouthpiece of a hookah in his hand. He had the face of an Eastern, yet moulded somewhat finely in the features; and his jet-black hair hung in ringlets upon his shoulders. His robe was woven in one piece, —a robe of purple silk, —but there was no turban on his head, and his legs and feet were bare but for slippers studded with gems. Jewels shone from rings on his hands, and his one woven vestment was bound about him at the girdle with a cincture of fine linen studded with diamonds. A quaint figure and impressive; a mind not lacking thought or purpose, I surmised, and something kindly in the black eyes which then looked upon me.

"Son, I give you greeting," he said, "and thanks that you wait upon me."

"The thanks are yours," I replied. "To drink that wine is to live."

"It is good wine," he said thoughtfully; "and good wine is one of the factors of life-blessed be him that made it!"

"It is new to me as an Englishman," I answered; "and if I were not a stranger to you, I would ask questions."

"Son, he that asks questions is a poor learner; ask nothing from life, but take it as it comes to you. He that asks shall learn lies."

"You are a philosopher, I see."

He laughed scornfully in reply.

"la philosopher! Nay, my son, I am no philosopher. I am the concentration of life, which I have squeezed as you squeeze a lemon, until it has poured its last drop into my skin-blessed be he that made it!"

"Wonderful man! You have learned, then, to live, and you keep the secret to yourself?"

"Nay, not so, since you are here to share it. I have waited for you many days until I could give you what you wished; for what you wish is another factor of your life. To-night it is in my power to put before you the realization of the dream which has been in your mind the month past. I intend to do so without condition; for condition is not an element of satisfaction, though made one by your teachers here, who would have no sustenance or employment if limitation were not part of their gospel. To-night you are my guest in the secret of pleasure as in the freedom of my house; and again I give you greeting."

He said the words, putting his hand upon an ivory knob in the floor beside him, when of a sudden the hundred silver lanterns about him slowly waxed radiant with a soft rose light that fell upon us and lit the scarlet and the gold of the tapestries so wonderfully wrought. I knew not until that time how large that chamber was, and I fell to wondering what sort of house it was which possessed such an apartment, and where it lay. But I had small opportunity to wonder, for at the lanterns' light there was the sound of distant music, and a surpassing strange sensation of singers and dancers near to me, yet all invisible. I was conscious only of a movement of the warm and perfumed air and of the presence of women surpassingly lovely, though unseen by me. The spirit-music, too, was entrancing beyond all music that I have heard-harmonious in its discordance, message-bearing, sensuous music, by which the walls of cities might have been built. Again, it was a sensation, and not a grasp of mathematical sound. I heard, and was not sure that I heard; I shut my ears, and yet was moved; hearkened for melody, and yet took none to me. But the delight was transcendent, indescribable; and I lay ravished, troubled as a woman in the ecstasy of her love. And he who had made the sign watched me, inhaling a thin vapor from the amber bowl, drinking of the cup which was at his hand.

The music ceased suddenly with a mad crash of strings. The man who sat before me pressed again upon the knob, and doors burst open in the wall behind him. I was conscious that a woman veiled in gauze, but whose rounded limbs showed pink and white beneath the veiling, was bending before him, and anon others, like dressed to her, spread meats at our feet. The old man made a sign to them, and they withdrew; but to me he spoke not, only pointing at the dishes as he cast the amber behind him. Then, too, I ate of the meats, which were cut in portions as the size of toast dressings, but had a flavor most curious and unknown to me. I found that so much as one mouthful had satisfied my hunger, but had produced a prodigious thirst, slaked only in many draughts from the goblet, which was deep and long- bodied. It was new tome thus to dine, and I asked him whose guest I was and what kind were the meats which he had set before me.

"Son," he said, "the guest asks not of the host, What do I eat with thee? Nor does he who would dine waste his moments on words which have been said by others, and better said. As you are a stranger, I make light of your fault; but hark to this; When you shall know how to live you shall know also that man, who has labored two thousand years and more to learn the things of life, has given not one year to learn of those things which are of the essence of life. He remains as the beasts, taking the fodder of the field, and where food should be his idol be has no reverence for it. Eat you, then, as the wise who have found light."

But I was satisfied, and could eat no more. The drink in the goblet, too, swayed me in a paroxysm of sensuous ecstasy. The room seemed a very bower of rose light. The jewels sent myriads of rays dancing toward me and blinding the eyes. Again the music arose, again he who ate touched the knob at his side, and the door in the wall of tapestry flew open. I saw the figure of a woman pass in, she veiled as the others had been; but she passed on to my side, and drawing back the veil, showed a face wondrous fair.

It was the face of Lelia, for whom I had waited so long at the theatre.

Part III-The Seven Men with the Seven Sands

When the pleasures of the lantern-room had continued three days, it came that the third night fell, and a deep sleep held me. Many hours passed, and I lay in a trance,—the trance of living death,—knowing nothing even of dreams, nor of that consciousness of rest which waits upon a brain yet active. I awoke at length, to find myself alone and in another chamber. A soft light-the dim light of day-fell from a rose window in the ceiling of the room, but there was no other aperture, and I could not distinguish any visible door which gave access to the place. For my own part, I lay upon a low bed, whose curtains were of silk, and I saw that an ivory table at my side had meat and drink upon it; but it was not the food which I had tasted when the old man served me, nor was the wine dream-giving as the wine of the other time.

For many hours I lay, suffering much from a weakness which had come upon me in waking, and I set myself to ask for the first time what the meaning of this strange adventure might be. Into whose hands had I fallen, and for what object? Who was this old man who had troubled himself to gratify my pleasures and to satisfy my wishes? What recompense did he ask? and in what way would the affair end? That there was danger in my position I did not doubt in my cooler moments, for, if all were well, for what object had my long-eyed host thus isolated me! I knew that I had been in the house at least three days, and a great longing came upon me to be out in the world again. I remembered that there would be many to ask for me, that engagements awaited me, that I had my pretence of business to attend to; and, above all, I began to long to fly from these rooms of darkness, from the perpetual night, from the perfume-laden atmosphere. And yet I was in a room the walls of which seemed impenetrable—a room without door or window—a room which was a well-furnished prison I did not doubt. This knowledge moved me to action, and I sprang from the bed, determined to ascertain the truth.

Now, at the moment when I rose, a curious thing happened, for the curtain of blue in the right corner of the chamber, which had seemed a perfect whole, divided in half, and a man with one hand stood before me. He was dressed in a long white garment, shaped as an alb, and girded at his waist, and was altogether as an Eastern, though his face was as the face of our people. I saw that he was young, but lines furrowed his cheeks, and he was deadly pale, with the pallor of a man who is shut from the air of life. Nor did he seem to see me when he moved to the table and laid upon it a small casket in pure gold; only he raised his voice, and said, in loud tones"

"Son, three days are numbered and three nights are numbered. Rise, and go hence, or be for all time as I am."

Then he left the room as he had come, and I looked behind the divided curtain to see that the wall had opened, and that a long passage lay beyond it—a passage leading into a garden where flowers bloomed. The temptation to greet the sun and the God-given air was immense; but I stayed a moment to open the casket upon the table, and stood still with astonishment as I looked upon its contents. There, on a little bed of wool, lay a ruby, large and lustrous as the finest from Burmah, and a little scroll of gold above it had the words, "Son, who would live must lack." I knew not the whole meaning of the fable, but it appeared that my host wished to make a trial of me; and I determined to go, showing him that I had mastered self and passion. And so I took up the jewel and passed into the garden. But what a wondrous sight there met my eyes! The whole air seemed deep-laden with the richest perfumes, vast shrubs towered up into the high roof of glass above, fountains played, and rare birds sang. There, too, in the very centre, was a great bath of marble, and as the cool of the glittering water spread about, I determined that I would bathe, and go out into the day refreshed.

I had come out of the bath, and wrapped about me one of the robes of linen which hung upon the rail of ivory, when I saw beneath a canopy of silver cloth another cup of wine, standing upon a table, and a couch spread under the leaves of a tree whereon luscious fruit was hanging. What madness took me I know not, but the bath seemed to have fatigued me, and I drank of the wine, and ate of the fruit; yet I had scarce put it to my lips when another man with one hand stood before me, and laid a casket upon the table as the other had done. He, too, cried with doleful voice, saying:

"Son, three days are numbered and three nights are numbered. Rise, and go hence, or be for all time as I am."

I opened his casket and found that it contained a great opal, and a scroll whereon these words were written: "Son, what is all is not all; and what is not all is all." But the meaning was hidden, as the meaning of the other fable; and I began to laugh at the warning as the wine exhilarated me, and to lose inclination to leave the garden of delights and the draught which was life. Indeed, for some while I lay upon the couch of silk and skins, listening to the hours as they were chimed upon a great, sphinx-like clock above me; and as each hour was numbered, it seemed to me that a new man with but one hand stood by me, and cried:

"Son, three days are numbered and three nights are numbered. Rise, and go hence, or be for all time as I am."

And each laid upon the table a casket and a gem, until five were added unto the number which I had—a turquoise, a pink pearl, a black pearl, a diamond, and an emerald; and the five scrolls had these five warnings:

"Look not to reap in the season of the sower."

"When the end cometh seek not to begin."

"Behind thee is thy future; before thee is thy past."

"Mind not matter, if matter be less than mind."

"There is time for all things save for death."

Now, when the Seven Men with the Seven Hands had left me, I thought at length to go forth from the tent, and rose up to dress myself again, and to take away the jewels of price which had come to me so curiously. But as I rose, Lelia, whom I had not seen that day, came of a sudden to the spot, and I drew her to me, wondering at her beauty, which was yet more dazzlingly fair in the garden of delights. And I would have questioned her of herself, and of this strange home of hers, and of a hundred other mysteries as she sat upon the couch at my side. But when I so much as began to speak, and to question her if she would leave the place and follow me, that I might not again be separated from her, she put her hand upon my lips to hush me, and held me tight in her arms so that her hair fell upon my shoulders and her face was close pressed against my breast. Then she begged me to leave her, saying that the end must come, and the better if it should be in that moment. Nay, she implored me to say nothing, nor to delay; "for," said she, "if you do not go now, you may never go, and that shall bring no happiness to you or to me." But how could I leave her in that house of light, knowing not if I should see her or even hear of her again? Through many long months I had waited for her, had watched the lustre of her dark eyes, the beauty of her exquisite figure, the silk-knit waves of her lovely hair that fell upon her shoulders; and at last I held her to me, felt her kisses warm upon me-and she willed that I should leave her! Do you wonder that I answered her with a deep seal upon her lips; with an embrace wherein all the joy of life seemed to be gathered? Alas! that it was the last embrace we knew-die whom I loved, the child of mystery.

As I kissed her thus, of a sudden she rose and tore herself away from me.

"Leave this place," she said, with a voice of fear; "leave it, or the hour will have passed; leave it, if you would see me again! I ask you, who may never ask again; go now, before the moments fly!"

And she left me as she had come. But I remained, drinking from the goblet, mystified and unnerved, until the bell of the sphinx-like clock rang out and the first hour of night chimed. I listened to the hour-it was seven o'clock; and the seventh stroke had not died away in echo when the tent under which I sat dropped upon me, and I felt its folds being bound about my body. It was the work of a moment, and I lay helpless as a log, bound hand and foot, and in black darkness. But I knew that men carried me, and I heard a door clang before silence fell.

Part IV-The Chamber of the Cimeter

They had uncovered my head from the folds of the silver-cloth when they laid me in the room, and they loosened the bonds of my body. I was unbound save at the left hand, which was chained-as I judged by touch-to a cube of iron. But all the room was dark, and I lay for many hours, cold and shivering, upon a floor of stone. When the light came at last it was from an arc lamp high above me, and I saw that my surmise had been right. I was in a cell of stone, bare and cold, without window or furniture, and my left hand was chained to a block of iron. But what brought a new chill to my heart, and damped my forehead with the sweat of fear, was the cimeter of steel which lay close to my touch. For what object was it placed there? With what purpose? Then I remembered the Seven Men with the Seven Hands, and cursed the place and him who had brought me there.

It was my thought at that moment that the men who had brought me to this cell would return anon and do their work upon me, but I lay long and was alone. Nor did I hear any sound or movement through the great mass of stone-not so much as a hum from the city or the fall of a foot. The silence bred a strange terror in me. I seemed in one moment to learn the whole purpose of the man who had been my host. I recalled the seven warnings he had given me, the words upon the scrolls, the repeated urging to curb the will and to fly. Here, then, was a philosopher and a devourer of men. He had offered me pleasure, he had offered me pain; I had chosen both when it lay upon me to take but the first; and now I was about to reap,. What said the Seven Men with the Seven Hands?

"Rise and go, or be for all time as we are."

For all time maimed and a servant in that prison! The thought tortured me. I swore that I would fight for my limb as none had fought there before. And I took the cimeter, which lay at my right hand. It was a weapon superb to see, shaped as the short swords of Japan, sharper than any razor of the

West; and upon the gold that bound the shark-skin of the scabbard I read the words:

"FREE THYSELF-OR BE FREED."

"Free thyself-or be freed." A new enigma, a word puzzle, a humor of the long-eyed man. How should I free myself? How be freed? I looked at the left hand bound to the block, and the answer came to me. I could only free myself by losing the hand; by severing it myself with the cimeter they had offered to me. Horrible thought! To be a self-maimer; to curse one's self to all time for the deed which the right hand did to the left! I shuddered, and the sweat of fear ran from me to the stone.

When many hours had gone, and I had put the thought from me, it came upon me again, and had taken strength tenfold to itself. "Or be forever as we are." The words haunted me; the spectres of the seven men were ever before my eyes. I crouched from them, and yet they fell upon me, pointing at the block. I shut my ears by will, and their words rang louder than before. I prayed to God to be delivered from the dead, and was mocked back by devils who said, "Free thyself, free thyself!" In my agony I rolled upon the floor as my chain would let me, and an all-absorbing longing for life and light and home came upon me. To be for ever amongst the halt and the maimed, the scoff of whole men, the jeered of women! And to be so by an act of self! No mad terror of night was as this terror, no phantom dream as this reality. Hours must have passed-days, perchance-and still I lay chained, the cimeter in my right hand, the other bound. I kissed the fingers of the doomed hand madly, hugged the arm which they prompted me to maim, grew delirious with joy as 1 knew it remained to me. But my strength of reason was going; the longing for freedom was becoming stronger; the will to resist weaker and weaker, until at last, as the frenzy took me, I raised the gleaming blade, and with one powerful stroke laid my left hand upon the stone.

I was free! and as the blood ran I fell back fainting on the floor.

I regained consciousness in my own chambers in the Temple. I was lying in bed with my left hand bound, and my old servant waiting upon me. He said that they who carried me there talked of an accident in the street, and he asked me of what nature it was. I put him off with an idle tale, and took up the letter which had been left for me; but a curse fell from my lips when I found I could not open it, and remembered that I had but one hand. So he broke the seal, and I read the words: "*Son, seek in the East, and thou shalt find.*"

And from the well-sealed envelope there fell out the opal, the ruby, the emerald, and a diamond which was half the size of the diamond I had left in the garden. Then I knew the enigma, and that the day would come when I should meet the long-eyed man again. But it would be in the freedom of sacrifice, the freedom of the pain which I suffered then and after.

CHAPTER VI
WE MAKE READY THE WEDDING GARMENT

This was Connoley's story, just as he wrote it. Strange enough I never set eyes on the man after that time in Paris; and within a month from the day he gave us the paper we were in Derbyshire, and Sir Nicolas Steele was in a fair way to do the best deal he ever did in his life. How it came about that fortune checkmated him once more I shall now try to tell, simply saying that while no man was ever more surprised than I was to find myself, after twelve months' exile, so to speak, again comfortably settled in a great country house, so was I sure from the start that the affair would never come to a head, and that Janet Oakley would never be Lady Steele.

We had been in Paris six months, living anyhow, but avoiding any thing which could remind London of our existence, when my master received the invitation, and determined to accept it.

"'Tis good luck entirely," said he, "for there will be no one in Derbyshire in July, and I'll be glad to see the back of these Frenchmen for a while. Bedad, 'tis possible that the old man will adopt me. He has a pretty daughter any way, and that's a good beginning."

I said nothing, though I thought that he ran some risk in going to England just then; and three days after we were at Melbourne station driving to the house of Mr. Robert Oakley, than whom there is no better horseman nor more honorable gentleman in all Derbyshire, or Europe for that matter. Nicky would listen to no advice at that time; nor did he answer my suggestions with any thing but a laugh.

"Indeed, and 'tis a ladies' school ye should have kept," he would say. "Ye're over fearful for any decent business, and that's a fact. Is it ghosts ye look to see when we're at the White House?"

I did not answer him, but I was still sure that we were wrong in leaving Paris, and when we had been Mr. Oakley's guests for a month, he had reason to think as I did. For it was then that we received the telegram I am going to speak about, and that I shall never forget. The moment it came into my hands I knew the game was up; and he didn't need to read many times to agree with me.

"Hildebrand," said he, when I went up to his room with it just after the first gong for dinner had struck, "what the devil are you pulling a long face about now? Man, I'd think from your countenance that you were come to wake and not to marry me. Is it a tale you want to tell in all the house?"

"No tale, sir," said I, "but what's worse than a tale—a bungle. And you won't blame me, I'm sure. It was done against my advice all along. Now you see what's come of it."

He took the telegram in his hands and sat, half-dressed as he was, upon the bed to read it. I don't think, even then, that he understood it at all, for he looked it up and down, and turned it over and over, just as if there was more written upon the back of it.

"Well," said he at last, "and if I can make heads or tails of it, put me in Hanwell!"

"Then you don't read it properly, sir," said I; "can't you see that it's not for me at all?"

"Then whom, pray, is it for?"

I took the telegram and read it to him. It was in these words: "Return to Datcham at once-meet you there." But there was no signature nor any mark that would have betrayed the sender.

"Now, sir," said I, holding the message still in my hands, "isn't it plain to you?"

"Be hanged if it is!" said he.

He was always a very poor thinker, was Sir Nicolas Steele, but that night he was stupid beyond ordinary. I had no patience with him, and yet, goodness knows, it was not a night for temper.

"Look, sir," said I, "it's all as plain as the signboard of an inn. That telegram is meant for Lord Heresford, over at Altenham Lodge. There's been a bungle at the post-office, and what was meant for him has come to me, while, likely as not, what was meant for me has gone to him."

He saw it now, and his face went white as a sheet.

"Then," said he, "you think that he'll get to know we are here?"

"That depends upon what my telegram said. Better to have sleeping dogs lie, sir. We might have lived here a month just as snug and safe as aboard your own yacht. And it was any odds you'd have got through without talk-leastwise until the wedding was done."

He heard me testily, beginning to dress himself anyhow, just as he always did when trouble was at our heels.

"Well," said he, after some time, "that may be all true, and he may come here; but what then, Hildebrand, what then?"

"Ah! that's for you to say, sir. It seems to me that we shall want a change of air again. He is not a merciful man, is Lord Heresford-and this isn't the first time he's bundled us out neck and crop, as you know well."

"As I know well-confound him! But what if I wouldn't go? what if I snapped my fingers in his face? You can't forget the wedding's for Saturday, and this is Wednesday night. Is it in two days that he's to confirm his word? Bedad! I've the best of him any way, bring what tale he may."

"Sir," said I, now quite angry with him, "that's child's talk. Do you forget Margaret King so soon? You may, but he's a longer memory."

He sat down on the bed again, but he looked for all the world like a broken man. If there was one word to bring Sir Nicolas Steele to his senses, it was mention of Margaret King, and the trouble that had come with her.

"Hildebrand, Hildebrand," said he, "'tis a mortal unlucky man I am, for sure. To think that Heresford of all others should be here in Derbyshire, and me wanting three days to my marriage! What we're to do, Heaven knows!"

"It's late to talk of it," said I, "for, if he's coming, he'll be here with the morning-and we'll be on the road before this time to-morrow. Let's hope for the best, sir. It's just possible there was nothing in the other telegram to set him thinking."

"Is that likely?" he asked eagerly.

"It should not be," said I; "my brother's no fool, and this is no mistake of his. But he wouldn't have looked for Heresford of all others to read what was meant for me. What I'd better do, sir, is to go down to the village at once and get the other telegram. You, meanwhile, put a good face on it. We shall want all that before we've done."

"That's true," said he, in a very melancholy voice, "but I'd have given a thousand to have pulled this affair off. She's a sweet little woman, for sure. Bedad, 'tis the devil's own luck that's with us, upon my life!"

"Indeed, and it is, sir," said I, "and our own fault, too, I'm thinking. It was never my idea that you should try to get Lord Heresford out of Derbyshire."

"Faith, you speak true. If we'd have let him alone, we'd be right as a trivet now. And Saturday gone, we might have snapped our fingers in his face. Well, well, it's my own fault. I've just a poor head for scheming, Hildebrand, and that's the plain fact. But I count upon you. You'll go down to the village at once?"

"I'll be down and back again while you're at dinner, sir," said I.

"And if your brother said nothing compromising — —"

"In that case you're as safe here as anywhere. But I'm doubting that he didn't."

"You're quick to make the worst of it," said he very gloomily; and with that I left him to finish his dressing.

It being dinner time, there were few about the place to take any notice of my doings; and I slipped through the park, and so, by the long drive, to the Melbourne Road without a word to any man. Though it was late in July, the evenings were long-drawn, and when I stood upon the hilltop, the windows of the old house below seemed ablaze with the red light of the sun. I could see Mr. Robert Oakley and his daughter waiting in the garden, as I thought, for Sir Nicolas; and while I stood a minute to watch them, I realized for the first time the whole of our misfortune.

"Three days more," said I to myself, "and rogue or no rogue, Sir Nicolas, you could have stood with any man in that house. But who knows now where you will be this time to-morrow night? under lock and key, perhaps, or in the train for Paris? Oh, Fortune, Fortune, what a slut you are!"

I said this to myself, turning out of the lodge gate, and giving "good-night" to the keeper. It seemed only a week ago since we had driven up that same drive, and had been received by Mr. Oakley and his daughter just as if we were princes. And yet it was a month or more, and we had lived that time with never a man to come up to the White House-for that was the name of Mr. Oakley's place-to tell them that they had better make enquiries about their guest. A fine gentleman, as I have said, was that Mr. Oakley. We'd met him two winters back at Cannes, where my governor's riding caught his eye, as well it might, for there is no better horseman breathing than Nicky Steele. The friendship was warm from the first. Mr. Oakley was no man of the world, and knew nothing of what the world was talking about. And my master, like all Irishmen, had the gift of the gab. Talk! you'd think he was a boy of eighteen, and not a man hob-nobbing with the tail end of the thirties, as I know he must be. And it was no surprise to me that the young lady-Miss Janet her name was-stood friends with us so quickly. She'd lived all her life among boobies; and here was a man who knew every city worth the knowing, and could tell her tales of half the people in Europe. I said to myself often when I saw them walking in the old garden together—"Nicky, it really does look as if we're to be settled for life this time," and indeed I could not help but think we were to pull it off, the way things were going at the White House. So far as I knew, there was not a creature in the county who could say any thing about us. Mr. Oakley himself would listen to no gossip. He liked my master's boyish frankness and big-hearted ways. And if ever Sir Nicolas Steele was hard hit by a girl, it was by Janet Oakley.

Unbelieving as I was, all these things had half persuaded me that my master was right and I was wrong, for all went smooth and the day was fixed, and what was to be put in the papers was given to me, who lit my pipe with it. From the first we had stipulated for a quiet marriage, for my master pretended that he had just lost his only brother, who died at Castle Rath, County Kerry,—he really died three years ago, but our grief was still young,—and being in mourning, he asked for a plain wedding, with a few county folk to see him off, and neither ball nor party to make a splash. Mr. Oakley didn't much like this, for it was a boast of his that he would fill all Derbyshire with "sixty-three" port when his daughter married; but he gave way to Sir Nicolas, and the affair was kept as quiet as possible. This was lucky, since there were plenty who would have come all the way from London to make things pleasant; and for the matter of that, we'd have been hard pressed to fake up presents enough for a show. As it was, I had to buy a few little things in town and to send them down by my brother, Jerome Bigg; but the county folk rained plate and jewelry on Janet Oakley, and old Mr. Robert's gifts were worth two hundred and fifty to pawn any day.

Things were just in this way when the week-before the wedding arrived. I remember the Saturday night well-how Sir Nicolas told them that he had sent instructions for bonfires on all the hills in Kerry; and how, notwithstanding his young brother's death, his people were coming to the castle by hundreds to drink a bumper to Janet Oakley. He was always good to play the winning game, was my master; and that we were winning hand over fist at the White House no man could deny. Once married to that rosy-cheeked miss, who knew no more of the world than a child of seven, Sir Nicolas might have laughed at his friends. That old Oasley would have stood by him I did not doubt, if once the thing were done. And when that night I saw Janet kissing her husband that was to be on the stairs leading to the picture gallery, I said to myself, "Kiss away, miss, for there'll be tears to follow, quick enough."

I'd been pretty busy during the day, beginning to get my master's clothes ready for the following Saturday. It was near to twelve o'clock at night when I sat down to a glass of whiskey and water and a pipe, and to a copy of a local paper left by the butler in my room. This I read a while, and it was when I was running my eye over the fashionable intelligence that I saw the news about Lord Heresford. They said he was staying at Altenham Lodge,—the Earl of

Holford's place, about ten miles from us,—and when I read the paragraph my heart jumped just as if it was coming into my mouth.

"Good Lord!" said I, "what a thing for a man to read!" For, you see, of all men in Europe I'd least soon have met in Derbyshire, Lord Heresford was the man. He knew well enough the whole history of the Margaret King affair; he knew why we left Dublin suddenly two years ago. Just as Sir Nicolas hated him-and Nicky could hate a man-so he hated us. I didn't doubt that he'd come a hundred miles to show us up, and here he was in Derbyshire, and we wanting a week of the marriage. The devil himself couldn't have dealt us shabbier luck.

I must have sat on my bed two hours, thinking what was to be done. After all, it seemed to me that we should be better advised to leave the matter alone. If Heresford had been in Derbyshire a week without scenting us, why should he not remain another week? Any way, we could do nothing to move him; and I saw that any word of us might bring a hornet's nest about our ears.

"You leave it alone, sir," said I to Sir Nicolas next morning; "just go on as you are. But don't be driving about the county, and when you ride, let it be in the park here. That's all the advice I can give you."

"'Tis precious bad luck any way, Hildebrand," said he, "and I don't know that we oughtn't to do something. You don't forget that he's only eight miles from here. He'll not be remaining another week and know nothing of us. Faith, that would be a miracle."

"It's the best course, sir," said I; "let sleeping dogs lie, as I've often told you. Eight miles in the country are eight miles. How should he hear of you now if he's not done it by this time?"

He was not satisfied, and all the Sunday he thought of it. There are few who would call Nicky Steele a coward, but this Heresford was like a whip to him. He lost his laugh that day, and for the most part he spent the hours in his bedroom. When I went up to him at night, he had made up his mind, and nothing that I could say would turn him from his purpose.

"Hildebrand," he cried, "we must get this jabbering old idiot out of Derbyshire, and we mustn't lose time about it."

"Will you please to tell me how that's to be done, sir?" I asked.

"To be done, man-you've no more wits than a pig"—he always spoke impatient like this; "why, fetch him back to his place at Datcham with a telegram. Isn't that how it's to be done? Look, now, the wedding's for Saturday-this is Sunday. Let your brother wire to him on Wednesday from London. No name, of course, and no address. Just the simple words—'Return home at once.' That 'll fetch him to Surrey on Thursday, and before he's time to think of it we'll have done the trick. Faith, 'tis a good idea, too, and lucky that one of us did not leave his wits in Paris. Why, man, a child could see it."

I did not argue with him, hoping to find him in better mind next morning; but the more he thought of it, the more he liked the idea, and so it came about that on Tuesday he had his way, and I wrote to my brother Jerome in London telling him to telegraph to Heresford at Altenham. But it was my notion to add the words—"meet you there," for, said I, that will put him off the scent, and he will think that his lawyer or some one wishes to see him on big business. In this way the whole telegram would read, "Return to Datcham at once-meet you there," and might after all, I thought, help us over a stiff place. Any way, I posted the letter to Jerome on the Tuesday in time for the London post, but it was not until the Wednesday evening that the answer came, and hit us, so to speak, fair between wind and water. I saw what had happened directly I looked at the thing. Either Jerome had addressed his telegram wrongly, or the muddle was made at the post-office. Be that as it might, I had got the message intended for Heresford, and he must have got the message intended for me.

"Now," said I to myself, as I went down the village road that night, "was ever such a thing heard of-that we should go out of our way to bring that old busybody buzzing about the White House? And just when we seemed set for the best innings we'd ever played! It's enough to make a man cut his throat."

CHAPTER VII
OLD BARKER SHOWS HIS BOOKS

All this, as you may think, was in my mind when I set out for the post-office to find out, if I could, what message really had been given to Lord Heresford. I knew well enough that a word would send him barking to old Oakley; and if that word had been written, good-by to Miss Janet, said I, and heigho for Paris again. This wasn't the first time by a long way that Nicky and I had changed our quarters suddenly; but better quarters than the White House we couldn't hope to find in a hurry-better quarters nor better people, for there wasn't a man of them, even down to Reubens, the constable, that didn't treat us in slap-up style. Whenever I went into the village, it was "Good-day to you, Mr. Bigg. Ye'll take a glass of ale with me?" or, "How's Sir Nicolas finding himself to-day, Mr. Bigg? Been riding, I suppose. Ay, he's a wunner on horseback is your master." Strange, it was, too, how they did love Nicky, every man, woman, and child among them; and this I will say, that more pleasant manners with children you'll never see this side of Dublin.

When I got down to the post-office, old Barker, the post-master, was at the meeting-house, "wrestling with the Lord," his wife called it; and there was nothing for it but to catch him as he came out and before he got into the public. But I hadn't been in the village five minutes when Reubens came sidling up to me, and began a parley. He was a rare talker, was Reubens, and if you wanted any thing put abroad, you couldn't do better than give him a whisper of it.

"Evenin', Mister Bigg," said he. "I do hope that you be finding yourself better this day."

"Well, thank you, Mr. Reubens," said I, "it's not much that I'm complaining of. Will you have a cigar to-night?"

I offered him my case, and he took a smoke readily.

"It's funny," said he, biting off the end of it then and there, "that you should be offering me bacca, for it weren't five minutes ago that Mrs. Reubens says to me, 'Reubens, ye're more tiresome this night than I can remember. Drat ye, go out and smoke your pipe, and leave me to get the childer to bed.' Ay, wunnerful woman she is with childer! Ye'll not be having a lucifer about you, Mr. Bigg?"

"Oh, but I have, though. You'll take a glass of ale with me, Mr. Reubens?"

"Well, now, you do put things into a man's head!"

I took him up to the Duke of York, and we went into the private bar at his wish.

"There's some as say," he explained, "that a constable shouldn't go for to be seen drinking in a public; but that's not my word. A man's a man, and no' the worse for taking a glass of yale like other folk. And it's example, too. What would ye think of a policeman that wanted a stomach for a sup of beer? That's no man to preserve the Queen's peace."

"Quite right," said I. "But I don't suppose the Queen's peace wants very much preserving in these parts."

"No," said he, draining his jug at a draught; "we're a tidy civil folk as folk go. When there's trouble, it's a'most a' ways brought by strangers. An' that reminds me-ye'll not have been looking for any man from Lunnon to-day, Mr. Bigg?"

"What sort of a man?" said I, feeling a bit queer at the question; which was no wonder, remembering the business I'd come down to the village about.

"Spare party, with short legs and a fly-away voice," said he. "Clerkish way he has, too, pryin' about just as if he was sorting out pigs. Thought he might be down here about Saturday. Ay, but you'll be busy enough without him. She's a fine lady, is Miss Oakley; no finer in the county, that I do say. And I've seed a many giv' and took since I was a lad, Mr. Bigg."

"That's so, Mr. Reubens," replied I; "you must have seen a wonderful lot in your time. But this clerk, now-was he asking after me?"

"After you-no; I don't mind that he was, or I'd have been bringing him up to the house. Queer party he is, though. And you'll not forget that there are diamonds and such up yonder now. There's been stranger things in Derbyshire than house-breakers, Mr. Bigg."

I saw in a minute what he meant, and I could have burst out laughing in his face. When he told me that a clerk was in the village he didn't need to say more. I knew well what the chap was after, and I said to myself, "Nicky, my boy, here's another bit of white paper which the wind has sent us." Yet how they had scented us out, or whose writ it was, I couldn't think. At the same time, it wasn't for me to be putting thoughts into the constable's head, and I kept my wits about me.

"It seems to me that the village should think itself lucky to have such a man as you about, Mr. Reubens," said I, after a bit. "There's no knowing what these London chaps aren't up to nowadays. Do you remember when old Lord Ramer was married down Bedford way last autumn? Well, the very night he was honeymooning, three of them entered his place and filled themselves right up with plate and jewels. Broke into his dressing-room, they did, and wired all the park, so that when his butler went after them he cut his face cruel. What do you think of that?"

"Ay, but it was bad business, Mr. Bigg."

"You're right there; and if I was you I'd keep my eye on this chap you speak of. Likely enough he's news of what's going on yonder. But I don't doubt you'll be good enough for him-and more to come."

This, you see, I said, to please him; and mighty pleased he was at it, giving me trouble to get away to the post-master. But I was itching to read the telegram which had gone to Heresford, and when he had drunk another glass of beer we went across to the post-office together. Old Barker was back from his hymn-singing now, and he made haste to light up his lamps and to refer to his book. It wasn't ten minutes before he'd come across the other message, and no sooner had I cast my eye over it than I knew the game was up.

"Have wired the old boy as directed. What is Nicky up to now?"

Here was the telegram I read, and pretty bad it made me feel, I must say. How my brother Jerome could have been such a fool, the Lord only knows; but there were the words, and I knew that Heresford must already have seen them.

"There's been a mistake here," said I to Barker, keeping as cool as I could. "The telegram you sent up to me was meant for Lord Heresford."

"You don't say so!" cried he, running hurriedly to the book. "Dear, dear, what an annoying thing to happen, Mr. Bigg!"

But I was wishing already that I had bitten my tongue off before making such a fool of myself.

"Well, perhaps it's my mistake," I cried, as quickly as I could. "But this wasn't the telegram I was looking for, that is all. You're quite sure that the words came over the wire as you have written them, Mr. Barker?"

"Just as sure as mortal man can be, I took them down myself. Not that I'm any Pope of Rome, Mr. Bigg, and above mistakes."

"No, that you bain't, Barker," said Reubens; "no more ain't we all. So long as the world is, so long will some of us go queer in the head when the weather's hot. Let's hope as there won't be no mistakes when our books is balanced upstairs. It 'ud be hard on a man to find himself in hell for the want of a bit of good summing."

"That's true," said the postmaster, and he said it very solemnly. "But I'll trust in the Lord's books, Mr. Reubens."

I listened to the two fools wrangling together for some minutes, and then it occurred to me that I ought to get back to the house again. I'd stopped long enough to put my foot into it pretty badly, and long enough to know that nothing but a miracle could marry Sir Nicolas Steele to Janet Oakley. It was bad enough when Heresford received the first telegram; but I saw-and I could have bitten my hand because I'd done it-that I had put him in the way of getting the second message, which must tell him as plain as a book what the matter meant. "Like enough," said I, "he'll be over here with the post to-morrow, and then where shall we be?" Upon my word, it was the crudest bit of business that I'd met with in the ten years I'd been man to Sir Nicolas Steele.

CHAPTER VIII
THE BEST MAN LOSES

It was quite dark when I came up to the White House. Old Mr. Oakley was snoozing in his arm- chair; Sir Nicolas was with Miss Oakley in the garden. I didn't mean to tell him any thing until he went up to bed; but he heard that I was back, and he sent for me to come out to the summer-house to him. When I got there, he was standing in the doorway of the arbor, with Miss Janet hanging on to his arm, as pretty a little thing as a man might find between London and Vienna.

"Well, Hildebrand," said she, "and I hope that you've brought me something nice from the post-office?"

"And I do wish I had, to be sure, miss," said I.

"Are they talking about Saturday in the village?" she went on, giving Sir Nicolas a good squeeze with her arm, as I could see.

"Doing nothing but talk of it, miss," I said. "There's to be fine doings down there when you're gone away. Mr. Oakley's a kind-hearted gentleman, I must say."

She didn't answer me now, but turned to my master, and cried:

"What do you say, Pat?"—like the other, she always called him Pat, because he was an Irishman, I suppose. "What do you say? Don't you think that we ought to stop and see the fun? Doesn't the thought of a roasted ox tempt you? We could dance on the green, you know."

He answered her with a laughing look, and just touched the top of her head with his lips. Never, I think, was Sir Nicolas so far gone with any woman as he was with Janet Oakley, and I knew by his way that he'd fight strong before he gave her up.

"Did you find the letter I sent you for?" he asked me presently, and when he'd done looking at her.

"No, sir, I did not," replied I, knowing well that he meant to ask me about the telegram. "It seems to me that it's been delivered at the wrong address."

"Are we likely to get it back again?" he continued, meaning to ask me, "Are we likely to weather the mistake?"

"I fear not, sir," said I; and dark as it was I could see him bite his lip with vexation.

"What's it all mean?" cried Miss Oakley now. "Has that silly old Barker been losing your letters?"

"I fear he has," said Sir Nicolas, "or worse than losing them-he's been presenting them to other people."

"He's a dreadful person," said she, "so prim and old-fashioned. He always puts his gloves on to deliver a telegram. It's quite an event in his history. I am sure he enters it in his family Bible."

My master laughed at this, but it was a cold laugh, and I could see that he wasn't so easy, though he had to put the best face on it.

"It doesn't very much matter at all, Hildebrand," said he; "likely the thing will turn up in the morning. Any way, it's not worth the troubling about now."

With this he turned away, and they went together toward the dining-room, Mr. Oakley calling them from the window. I did not see Sir Nicolas again until he came up to his bedroom, and then he had drank more whiskey than was good for him. It was always a way with him when he was like that to turn round upon me; but I knew him too well to take notice, and I let him rave as much as he liked.

"If it hadn't been for that cursed brother of yours, we shouldn't be in this mess," he whimpered when he began to undress himself. "Faith, to think how near we've been to it!"

He went on like this for a long time, and then began to tell me that he wouldn't leave the house.

"If I go-hang me!" said he, hurling his boots to the other side of the room. " Is it for such a one as him that I'm to be packing again? No, by Heaven! I'll shoot him first. D'ye hear that,

Hildebrand? I'll shoot the man first! Who is he, to come barking here about my business? Will you tell me that, please?"

I didn't see fit to argue with him then, and when I had got him into bed. and put the razors out of his reach, I left him mumbling to himself, and went back to my bedroom to pack my few clothes.

"Bigg," said I to myself, "you're going to make a journey to-morrow. It may be that you're going to Brussels, it may be that you're going to Paris-but go you must; and where the ready is to come from, you don't quite know. Nicky couldn't rake fifty together to save his life, and you haven't got a shilling to your back."

Things were now in such a state that this question of money troubled me more than any thing. Look where I would, I didn't see how we were to get enough to keep afloat for a week on the other side; and when I remembered that we should have to cut in a hurry, things seemed as bad as they could be. That we must go, I never had a doubt. Once Heresford was in the house, Sir Nicolas Steele would leave it smart enough. It remained to see if the man would come.

You may imagine that I didn't get much sleep that night. It was six o'clock in the morning before I closed my eyes, and then I overslept myself by an hour, not going into Sir Nicolas' room until half-past eight. The others were already up, and what should I see from the staircase window but Reubens, the constable, talking to Mr. Oakley and his daughter on the grass by the lake.

"Hallo!" said I; "what's brought you here? No good to us, I'm sure." And with that to give me a twinge, I went into my master's bedroom.

He was already out of bed, waiting to be shaved; but I could see that he wasn't himself, for his hand trembled when I gave him his clothes, and he spoke very cool and calm like.

"Well," said he, "is it any letter you're bringing me?"

"Not a half a one, sir," said I.

"Then there's no talk down stairs as yet?" he went on.

"I haven't heard any," said I, "but Reubens, the constable, is on the lawn with Mr. Oakley, and they're busy talking."

"What can that be now?" he asked mighty eagerly.

"That's what I'm going to find out presently," exclaimed I. "There's a young chap in the village with more paper for us; perhaps he's come about him."

"So the hawks have scented us again," cried he, sitting in the chair to be shaved; "well, I don't care a crack for them. 'Tis this Heresford that's troubling me. If he's to come, Hildebrand, there should be word or message from him this morning."

"That's so, sir," said I; "if you hear nothing when the gong for lunch goes, you may make your mind easy."

"Otherwise, I suppose there's only one way."

"Only one, sir," said I.

He gave a great sigh, and let me shave him without a word. When I had done that, he bethought him all of a sudden of something that had troubled me the whole night through.

"Hildebrand," said he, "it's badly off for money I am, let me tell you. I've not fifty in the world. I was looking for Oakley's check to his daughter to get through Saturday."

Now, when he said this, something came quickly into my head that was not there before; and when I'd thought of it a minute, I told him.

"One thing you're forgetting, sir," said I; "there's the things which Mr. Oakley give you-you wouldn't be leaving them behind."

"What things do you mean?" said he; "not the girl's wedding presents?"

"Well, not exactly those, sir, but the things given to you. Gifts are gifts, and not to be taken back, I think."

"You scoundrel," said he, springing up from his chair with his fist clenched, "would you make a housebreaker of me?"

"I don't know," said I, quite calmly; "but one thing I would do, Sir Nicolas — —"

"And what is that, pray?" cried he, standing white with passion.

"Keep you out of the hands of the police!" I replied, while I turned to put his things away.

What he did when he heard this I don't know, since I had my back to him. But he said nothing for a long time, and when he spoke there was no more bluster about him.

"Hildebrand," cried he, quite quietly, "if you could find out what the constable's here for, it would help us, don't you think?"

"I'm going down to do that now, sir," said I; "there'll be time enough to pack your bag while you're at breakfast."

"To pack my bag-what do you want to do that for?" cried he.

"Against accidents," said I; "and while I'm talking about it, let me say that you'd be wise not to go far from home to-day."

He heard me out, and then turned away to the window. I could see that there were tears rolling down his cheeks, and I thought it was fortunate that one of us at least had more than the heart of a woman. But it wasn't the time to say that to him, and I went down stairs to find out, if I could, why the constable had come up to the house, and whether there was any message from Heresford. Lucky enough, I met Mr. Oakley on the landing, and I knew from his manner that we were all right so far.

"Ha, Hildebrand!" said he, "you're the very man I want to see. Reubens, the constable, has been trying to frighten me about those wedding presents down stairs. He seems to think there is a person in the village who is to be suspected. I tell him it is all nonsense. As if any one would rob my house!"

"Reubens has got hold of the wrong end of the stick this time, Mr. Oakley," said I, seeing in a moment what was coming; "the man he's troubled about is clerk to Sir Nicolas' lawyer, I'm thinking."

He laughed very hearty at this, and leaned over the banisters to tell Miss Janet what I'd said.

"Janet, Janet," cried he, "Reubens' burglar is a lawyer's clerk. Did you ever hear such a thing? I mast tell that at the breakfast on Saturday."

"Was he thinking, then, of taking the gentleman in charge, sir?" I asked.

"Indeed and he was. And that's not all. He wants me to send the valuable things over to the bank at Melbourne, lest they should be stolen by what he is pleased to call a gang from London. Bosh! say I; there's no gang from London that will get in here in a hurry."

"That I'm sure they wouldn't, sir," said I, thinking it precious lucky that I'd hit upon such a good lie. It would never have done to let him be frightened into sending the presents away.

"I'm glad you're of my opinion, Hildebrand," said he next; "we're too busy for burglars just now. Is Sir Nicolas up yet?"

"He's coming down in a minute, sir."

He left me, and began to climb the stairs two at a time, like a man of twenty, and I could hear him muttering "Lazy dog! lazy dog!" because, I suppose, my master was late for breakfast. But I went on into the servants' hall, saying to myself that I'd never had a luckier thought than the one about that writ-server. If Mr. Oakley had listened to Reubens, and sent the diamonds away, we'd have been in a pretty pickle. As it was, I knew he would leave them in the drawing-room, and, so long as they were there, we were not likely to want a railway fare.

It was now about a quarter-past nine o'clock. The morning post had come in, and I was sure there was no letter or telegram from Heresford—a thing I couldn't understand at all. "This man can't be so blind that he doesn't read the meaning of that telegram," I said; and yet it was strange that the morning passed and not a sign of any trouble could we see. Nicky himself, always ready to go up or down in spirits like a thermometer, was half-wild with joy about twelve o'clock, and you could hear his laughter all over the house. Then he went riding with Miss Janet, and when he came back at two o'clock, and there was still no word from Heresford, he looked like a man who had lost twenty of his years in an hour.

I shall never forget that day if I live until I'm a hundred. The times I walked to the lodge gates to see if any one was coming up the road; the starts I got every time the dogs barked and the bells rang. I was that bad by six o'clock that I couldn't sit a minute anywhere; and well as the thing looked, I positively dared not believe in our luck. "It can't be, it can't be," I kept saying to myself; "he must come; he will be here in five minutes, in ten; he will drive up before the clock strikes again." And this went on all the afternoon until six o'clock, the hour when I had arranged to drive down to Melbourne to bring a few of our things up from the station; and still we were safe.

It was a relief to me to get away from the house, and to find myself alone. They always lent me the old dog-cart when I wanted to go to the town, and I said that night that I'd go by myself, for I had so many bags to bring back with me. We used to take about twenty minutes to drive into Melbourne in the ordinary way, but I shook the old mare up a bit on that occasion, for it was a quarter-past six when I passed the lodge, and I meant to get back a little after seven to help Sir Nicolas to dress. It seemed strange to me to find myself on a Derbyshire road at all, for I looked to be on the way to Paris long before then; and even as I drove along, I kept asking myself if it was me that sat there or another. I'd thought so much about the whole thing that I was almost stupid with it.

"It can't be; it can't be!" I said over and over again. "Heresford would walk a hundred miles to put a spoke in Nicky's wheel. He's sworn to hunt him out of every city in Europe, and he's a man of bis word. He *must* come."

I had made up my mind to this before I'd left the White House a mile behind, and I hadn't gone two miles down the road before time proved me to be right. It came about in this way. I had just turned into the lane which they call the chestnut-grove, and had given the old mare a cut with the whip to send her along a bit, when, looking through the trees into the meadow, whom should I see but Lord Heresford himself, walking across the fields straight toward the White House. The thing was so sudden that for a minute I thought I had seen a ghost. But it was only for a minute. While my heart was beating like an engine, and something was singing away in my ears, I kept my wits; and almost by a sort of instinct I reined the mare back, so that she stood almost upon her hind-legs.

"Bigg," said I, "this is just a tight place. You've got to think, and lose no time about it. It's a race, Bigg, and the best man wins. He can't get up to the house in less than twenty minutes; you should be up in six. Cut for it, man; cut for it!"

I said this, and with the words on my lips, I whipped the mare round, and sent her flying up the road like a racehorse. I've handled some horses, but I never, to my way of thinking, put a beast along so fast as I put the mare that night. She was dripping wet when I drove her into the yard, and tossed the reins to William.

"William," said I, when he came out, "I've news for my master that won't wait. Keep the mare to. It won't be three minutes before I'm on the road again."

He opened his mouth at this, but I ran into the house, and bumping against the butler in the hall, I asked him where Sir Nicolas was.

"He's knocking the balls about in the billiard-room."

"And Mr. Oakley?"

"Oh, he's dressing!"

It couldn't have been luckier. I found Sir Nicolas bending over the billiard table; he laid his cue down when I burst in, and said:

"Well, what's fresh now?"

I told him in ten words.

"Good God!" said he; "and what are we to do?"

"Just this," said I, "get your hat and slip down to the bottom of the paddock. You can strike the road to Nottingham there. I shall be by in the cart in two minutes, and I'll pick you up."

"Is there no other course?" he stammered.

"Unless you wish to spend the night in jail," said I, "you must do what I say. You haven't ten seconds to choose-he's almost at the gate."

For a minute he stood to curse and stamp, while his face was as white as the paper I write on. Then he did as I told him; and when I had watched him cross the lawn, I slipped back into the hall and listened at the drawing-room door. The place was quite empty; of that I was sure, and there being no one about, for the others were dressing for dinner, I entered the room and looked round for the stuff.

"Gifts are gifts," said I, "and we've as much right to them as he has, especially to the shiners, which will go into my pocket. He may keep the plate, and welcome-but I don't leave those stones behind."

It doesn't take long for a man to fill his pockets with diamonds. I was all bulging out with what I'd got; and almost before I'd realized the whole thing, I was back in the dog-cart again.

"Do ye bring bad news?" cried old William, tossing me the reins.

"Precious bad," said I, "and likely to be worse before morning. I'm driving to the doctor's. Let her go, William."

He gave her a slap with his hand and we bounded down the drive; the last thing I saw of the White House being the pretty face of Janet Oakley as she stood before the glass in her dressing-room. I wonder to this day that I didn't cannon the lodge gates, so fast I went; but luck was with me, and directly I was out on the road I looked for Sir Nicolas. He was standing there all right, but I had another shiver when I saw that Heresford himself had just come up to the stile, and was getting ove'r it. The two men were face to face an instant after, and then Heresford turned on him.

"You hound!" said he; "so you've come to kennel here? Indeed, it's lucky for them that I heard of you, Sir Nicolas Steele."

He was going to say more, and Sir Nicolas, I think, was about to hit him, for the man had a hand at his collar. Then I thought it time to act. Raising my whip suddenly, I struck Heresford across the face with it, and he reeled back, half blinded, across the road. In the same moment my master made a spring for the step, and no sooner was he on it than I gave the mare a vicious cut, and she galloped like a wild thing down the road. But we could hear Heresford calling for help long after we had left him, and we never let the mare trot until dark had come down.

It was daylight next morning when the two of us walked into Nottingham, and so struck the Midland main line. We had left the cart a mile out of the town, turning the mare's head back toward Derbyshire, and letting her go where she pleased.

"Say what you like, sir," said I, "we've got to separate. You track north to Hull, where you'll get steamer to Southampton and so to Havre. I go direct to Paris, where we'll look to meet in a week."

"You think that they will follow us, then?"

"No. Oakley will hush it up for his daughter's sake."

"I could cut my throat every time I think of her," said he.

"You'll be better when you're on the sea, sir," said I; "and don't forget that the job's been worth a thousand to us."

"Will the stuff bring that?" he cried eagerly.

"Every penny of it," said I.

And with this I put him into the train for Hull.

CHAPTER IX
WE OPEN THE GOLDEN EGG

We had been back in Paris nearly two months when the strange business connected with the golden egg came about. There was a time when I was very glad that my master had something to occupy his mind; but that was at the beginning of it. By and by, I thought much as the rest of them did; and whether to laugh or whether to cry I really did not know.

For my part, I was not sorry to be in Paris. All said and done, it's a city for a gentleman to live in. High born or low, good man or bad, you may find your company there so long as the guineas rattle in your pocket. And when you've spent your bit, you'll still find your company. That's the way of it-either rich or poor, but no betweens; and no need to show your family Bible before you're on nodding terms with your neighbors.

"If you'll take my advice, sir," said I to Sir Nicolas, the week after the Oakley affair, "you'll stop here until it's time to move for Monaco. Folks will be coming back from the seaside in a month or so, and meanwhile we'll do no hurt to rest a bit."

"Indeed, and I believe you're right," cried he, "though what a man is to do in Paris these times I'd like to learn."

"You've more than a thousand pounds to spend, sir," said I, reminding him how well we had sold Janet Oakley's diamonds.

"That's so," said he, brightening up wonderfully; "there's a deal of spending in a thousand pounds. And I don't forget that Jack Ames is here. There should be fun while he stops, any way."

"Quite true, sir," replied I, "so long as you don't play billiards with him. Making bold to say it, he could beat you with his umbrella."

"No such thing!" exclaimed he. "I'll take fifteen in a hundred and play him for a monkey any day."

"I wouldn't, if I were you, sir," said I; "we've got to go steady a bit yet-don't forget that."

This made him serious, as any word about his position always did.

"Do you think they'll follow us?" he asked quickly, "or is it some news you've got in your head?"

"Neither the one nor the other. I've no news, and I don't think they'll follow us, sir. But this I do say, that I wouldn't let myself be heard of for a month or so, if you can help it. There's no telling what Heresford would do if it came to his ears that you were starring about."

"You're right there. I'm trusting that Oakley hushed the affair up. There's nothing about it in the English papers that I can see."

"And there won't be, if we go on as we're doing now."

"Exactly; that's what I mean to do. Would I be advertising myself on the hoardings? Is it a child in long clothes that I am, Hildebrand?"

I said nothing, for it was plain that he was working himself up into one of his tempers. He'd been hard enough to bear with since we said good-by to Janet Oakley; but Sir Nicolas Steele was worth five hundred pounds a year to me, one way and the other, and you can stand a bit of temper at that price. I knew that he would think over what I said to him, and so it turned out; for a month went and he lived like a parson. Then, all of a sudden, came the business of the golden egg-and that's the story I write about.

The affair happened quite suddenly, as I say. He had been to Trouville with Jack Ames, and had lost a good deal of money, I knew. Ames was a long-nosed painting man, who lived on what he could get by finding fault with other people's pictures. He had nice manners, though; and I will say that he was a wonder with a billiard cue. Many's the mug he's skinned in this very Hôtel de Lille. I could have cried every time I saw my master going up to the billiard-room with him-and yet a prettier pair to play a four-handed match you'd never find. Ames it was who introduced Sir Nicolas to the theatricals of the Bouffes Parisiens; and what with giving dinners here and picnics there, the thousand we had made in Derbyshire soon looked thin enough.

"Never mind, Nick, my boy," that Ames used to say when be came with some new thing in bis head —" never mind, Nick, my boy; we'll marry you to a rich woman one of these days. And then I'll buy your pictures for you, be hanged if I don't."

You see, the man knew where to get him; for if there was one thing Nicky Steele never could stand against, it was a compliment about the women. The most ordinary creature alive could turn his head with a word. I don't think a vainer man ever was born into this world. He'd clothes enough to stock a theatre; and when I saw him, as I did often, standing before his glass like a schoolgirl dressing for her first party, I could have laughed in his face. If ever Jack Ames wanted money of him, he'd wheedle him with some story of a female who was after his *beaux yeux*, as he called it. And there wasn't a woman he knew who didn't flatter him outrageously, and laugh at what she'd done when his back was turned.

Well, it was by some tale of a woman that Ames got him down to Trouville; he paying the expenses, you may be pretty sure. The pair were away about a week, and when they came back, I knew that a good deal of money had been spent. He was very down in the mouth, and talked about going to try his luck in America, and other stuff. He got to work on the champagne, too, and I began to have the old trouble with him.

"What am I doing here?" he raved. It was the first night he was back from Trouville. "What's to become of me, Hildebrand-me that was born a gentleman? Is it in a garret you'd see me die? I haven't fifty pounds in the world, as the Lord is my witness."

"Now, don't you think of that, sir," said I. "You're not the man to die in any garret. Have a little patience, and we shall hear of something. Luck's never failed us yet, and it's not going to now."

"That's what you're always telling me," he wailed. "Luck-what's luck done for me? Is it lucky I am to have no friend in the world? The devil take such luck!"

I put him to bed-we were then staying in the Hôtel de Lille, over on the south side of the river, which corresponds to our London Surrey side-and next morning he slept late. It had been arranged that he and Mr. Ames should breakfast together in the hotel, and then go for a day down to Fontainebleau —*à la campagne*, as the French call it. I had called him at nine o'clock, but it was ten o'clock before he got up; and while he was dressing, the waiter brought up one of the funniest parcels 1 have ever seen. It was very small, very neat, done up in very bright blue paper; but more strange than any thing else was its weight, which was extraordinary for such a little thing.

"It seems to me, sir," said I, "that somebody has been making you a present of a few bullets. I never handled any thing like that in my life."

He took it in his hand and weighed it.

"What the deuce can it be, Hildebrand?" exclaimed he; and with that he cut the string, while I pretended to be busy with his clothes. But I saw him open the box, and when he got through a deal of tissue paper, he came to a little golden egg, quite the size of a plover's egg, and exactly like one in shape.

"Well," said he, "if that isn't rum! Who the blazes will be sending me this?"

It certainly was a funny thing, and when he passed the egg on to me, I was just as puzzled as he was. There it stood, a plain bit of gold-as you could tell by its weight-and not a mark or sign to make the giver known or to tell why it had been sent.

"Perhaps there's a letter with it, sir," said I, "or one will follow it."

"Is it gold, do you think?" he asked next.

"It should be, by its weight; but I'll put a drop of acid on it and see, sir."

It was gold right enough. The acid showed us that; yet when we had made the test, we had done nothing to answer the question, Who sent it?

"Who is it, now," he kept saying, "that is sending me golden eggs? It would be a woman most likely. Of course that's it. There'll be some message or letter to follow this. No one would be such a fool as to send the thing anonymously. Didn't I tell you that our luck would change. Bedad! it's changed already. I'll have a bottle of champagne on this, Hildebrand; it should be worth that, any way."

"Better wait a bit and see, sir," cried I; "though it's a queer present, I do say."

Well, it was no good talking to him; he was that excited about it already that he would have had the wine if his last guinea had bought it. I've known him before now to crack a bottle of champagne when he found a horseshoe in the road; and he always was one to be up or down like an umbrella. The least thing would send him laughing or crying; and this queer present, coming at a time when the money was very low, was quite enough. By the time I'd got the champagne he was singing at the top of his voice. What's more, the golden egg was open, and as I put the wine on the table I caught sight of the portrait of a woman lying in the heart of it.

"So, sir," said I, "you've found out all about it?"

"Yes," said he, coming to a stop suddenly, "it's only a locket, after all. Open the fizz, will you? my mouth's like a sandhill."

Now, it seemed to me queer that he should be so silent about it, but he never did talk to me when a woman was in the case. And it wasn't for me to say any thing when he held his tongue. So I uncorked the wine, and was pouring him out a glass, when Jack Ames opened the door and walked straight into the room.

"Halloa," said he, "at it already, Nicky, my boy! What's fresh now, then?"

"There's nothing fresh that I know of," answered Sir Nicolas, quickly closing the locket; "is it ready to start ye are?"

"As ready as yourself. You're *not* going to leave the liquor like *that*, surely? Man, it would be a crime!"

"Get another glass, Hildebrand," said my master now, " and when you've done that, fetch me *fiacre*."

I went to do his bidding, and when I had filled Mr. Ames' glass I left the room and shut the door after me. But I took good care to clap my ear to the keyhole, and then I heard them talking.

"Jack," said Sir Nicolas, "there's the strangest thing happened that ever you heard of. I've had a present, my boy, not half an hour before you came in. Look at that now, and tell me what you think of it."

There was silence for a while after this, and I supposed that Mr. Ames was looking at the locket. But Sir Nicolas was the one who spoke next.

"Did ye ever see a sweeter face?" he asked. "Isn't it curious that it should come to me like that, with not a word or a letter? Indeed, and I think it's a very pretty mystery."

Jack Ames spoke now.

"You've the right to consider it that," said he; "do you happen to know who the lady is?"

"No more than the dead," replied my master.

"Then I'll take leave to tell you. She's the Baroness de Moncy, the wife of the late Ambassador to Portugal. Her husband died four years ago, and left her three hundred thousand pounds. Nicky, my boy, it's a lucky day for you. Where the devil did she see you, may I ask?"

"How should I know that, when I hear her name now for the first time? But you're joking with me, Jack."

"Me! truth, I'm not, as you'll soon find out for yourself. Eh, gad, Nicky, I can hardly believe it, though I'm right glad about it, old man, and here's my hand on it!"

What more he said I didn't hear, for it was time to get the cab for them, and they went off together in a few minutes, Sir Nicolas being that full of himself that his hand shook when he emptied his glass. As for me, I didn't know whether I was on my head or my heels, and stood for a long time acting like a fool, I make sure.

"The Baroness de Moncy," said I, "and worth three hundred thousand! Well, if this don't beat any thing. To think that he cut that Derbyshire lot to run into a thing like this. Did any one ever hear of such a thing?"

The affair was a blank mystery, and that was all about it. That a woman should send her picture to a man she had never seen was not the least wonderful part of it. It was the rum way she sent it, with- out note or word. I've seen a good deal of women one way and another, and they do act in a surprising manner sometimes, I must confess. But that one of them, who was a baroness, should send a gold locket with her portrait to Sir Nicolas Steele, fairly beat any tiling I'd ever heard of.

"Who is she?" I kept asking myself, "the Baroness de Moncy? I've heard the name somewhere. She isn't in Paris now, or I should have known of it. He must have met her at Trouville at a masked ball or something. He couldn't have known her, but she knew him-and here's the reminder. Did ever a man have such luck?"

With this in my head I went to his private drawer, where he'd put the locket away, and I had a good look at it. The thing weighed heavy enough to be gold twice over; but it was not until I had fingered it for ten minutes or a quarter of an hour that I found out how to open it. You did it by a press of your hand upon the top of the egg, and then it flew open sharp, like a matchbox. The portrait, which might have been called a miniature, I suppose, lay deep in the heart of it. It was the picture of a girl perhaps of twenty-six years of age, and I must say. that the prettiness of the thing fairly took my breath away. I'm not one to say much about the looks of Frenchwomen as a whole, but this creature was beautiful beyond compare. If I'd have hunted Paris for a month I could not have found her like-not one so elegant or with such hair tumbling about her shoulders as that picture gave her. And when I remembered that Mr. Ames had said she was worth three hundred thousand pounds, I could have cried at the luck that had come to us.

CHAPTER X
THE EGG IS BROKEN

I say "the luck that had come to us," but it is not to be thought that I lost my head over the business. I was not so young as to take all that a man like Ames said for gospel truth. Indeed, I spent the remainder of that day in the *cafés* and *brasseries* round about the Hôtel de Lille, trying to learn what I could about the Baroness de Moncy. The result was not such as I had looked for. A few knew of her by name as a lady of great wealth, who had a country house at St. Germain and another at Trouville. One man at the Café Rouge thought that he had seen her, but could not remember any thing about her looks. The tale was that she had given up society after the death of her husband and had gone to live in seclusion. But there seemed no doubt about the money part of it, and that was what chiefly concerned me. So long as there were guineas to rattle, what did it matter if a painter had laid it on thick, so to speak. We could put up with plenty of that if the price was right.

It was seven o'clock when I got back to the hotel. I saw at once that a letter lay on the table—a dainty little note in a big feminine scrawl; but before I'd time to look at it, in came Sir Nicolas and Jack Ames, and with them that pretty bit of goods from the Bouffes Parisiens, Mimi Marcel by name. They were in all in rare fettle, especially my master, who read his letter and then would have it that they should dine with him. I don't know that I ever saw him in better spirits in my life, and it wasn't until nearly two in the morning that I got him to bed. But he was ready to talk at that time, and talk he did like one o'clock.

"Bedad!" said he, "I don't know that I'll go to bed at all this night, Hildebrand. Was there ever such a lucky devil born as I am? And only yesterday I was thinking of cutting my throat!"

"I'm glad to hear you've good news, sir," said I.

"Good news! and that's all you would call it? Why, man, my fortune's made-made, I tell you! I'm to meet her to-morrow night at the Café de Paris. To-morrow night-think of that! And I was dancing with her at Trouville, and thought no more of her than of a *grisette* out of a drapery store-though she did say that I should have her picture. Oh, it's a famous turn, for sure! I'll be married within the month."

He went on for a long time like this, throwing his clothes about the place, and behaving as if he wasn't right in the head; nor do I believe he was at such times. There are some men who can't stand Fortune when she runs with them. He was such an one, and there's many a good thing he's spoiled for want of a bit of balance. I found it best not to take any notice of him when he was all cock-a-hoop like this; and I used to get him into bed as quickly as possible and leave him to talk to himself. You could hear him singing half the night through sometimes when he'd had a bit of luck; and on this particular night I don't believe he slept a wink. He was up and dressed long before the time for me to take his hot water, and he left the hotel at nine o'clock to go over to Mr. Ames' rooms. I saw no more of him all day until he came in to dress at seven o'clock; and he was then in one of his silent tempers. He didn't say one word to me about what he'd done, not a word about the meeting at the Café de Paris, nor of what time I might expect him bade But he put his clothes on as though his life depended on it, and went off in a *fiacre* when the clocks were striking half-past seven.

"All right, my man," said I to myself, when he was gone, "you hold your tongue now, but I shall hear enough and to spare about it when you come back by and by with the liquor in you. Meanwhile, I might do worse than take a stroll and see where you get to."

I had thought of doing this all along, for somehow I never could bring myself quite to believe in what I'd seen or heard. That there was a screw loose somewhere I was certain; and yet, if you had asked me to put my finger on the place, I couldn't have done it, not to have saved my life. Not that there was any thing strange in a Frenchwoman running after Nicky Steele. I hadn't lived with him for all these years not to know that. It's wonderful what a bit of a handle to the name will do for a man in Paris; and that Nicolas Steele was a baronet, all the judges in the land could not deny. Nevertheless, I got no real grip on the truth of Jack Ames' story about the Baroness de Moncy, and that's the plain fact of it.

It was nearly dark when I left the Hôtel de Lille and crossed the river by the Pont du Carrousel. Paris was pretty full, though it was only the end of September; and when I came up by the Palais Royal there was a number of people sitting out to have their dinner in the open. I'd made up my mind that I'd ask for Sir Nicolas at the Café de Paris, but without going in to see him; and this I did. But they told me that he had only just looked in for five minutes and had then left.

"Did he go alone?" I asked the man, who was about as civil as he could be.

"He went with a gentleman," was his reply.

"With a gentleman-you don't say that?"

"Certainly; they met here and left together."

Now, I didn't want to let him see that this astonished me; but, if I must tell the truth, it took the wind clean out of my sails.

"Who can it be that he's met?" I asked myself; "and why's he gone off with him? What becomes, then, of the story about this woman at Trouville, whose picture he's got in his drawer? Is it any plant of the police that he's walking into, like a fox into a trap? Seems to me something like it."

It may sound strange to hear it, but that was the first time such a notion had come into my head. Directly it was there, I could no more get rid of it than cut my hands off. It set my brain going like a clock, and I began to run over all the affairs we'd been in for the last two years, and to ask myself which one would bring us to a quarrel with the police of Paris.

"It can't be Oakley," said I, "for he's not going to make public property of his daughter's misfortune; that I do know. And it can't be Margaret King, for there's no extradition when a woman cries. And it isn't the Dublin Club, because you can't lay hands on a man in Paris for holding too many aces in Dublin. No, we're safe enough here so far as I can see; and yet-and yet — —"

The fact was that I could make nothing of it. I must have walked about Paris that night for an hour and a half, turning it over and over in my head, and yet getting no forrader. When I stopped at last, I was before the Grand Café; for what should I see there but Sir Nicolas Steele himself, sitting down before a dinner-table, with no others for company than Jack Ames and Mimi Marcel. There was no doubt at all about it. There he was as large as life; and what's more, he seemed as happy as a schoolboy just come out of school. And at that I shook my head and went straight home.

"Bigg," said I, "this beats you, and no mistake. Just you leave it alone and go on with your work."

Well, I tried to do as I said I would, and at midnight Sir Nicolas came home, talkative as usual, but with all his wits about him. He hadn't quite the spirits of the night before, though you couldn't call him depressed; and he went to his bedroom at once.

"Hildebrand," said he, "it's better quarters than a fifth in the Hôtel de Lille we'll be occupying this day next month."

"Indeed, and I hope so, sir," said I.

"Oh, but I don't hope so at all," he went on; "I make sure. We'll be in the Trouville then, and no need to think about the bill. Bedad! it's bills that make half the trouble in life."

"There never was a truer word than that, sir," said I.

"Isn't it me that knows it-me that has enough blue paper to furnish the whole of this same hotel? But I've done with that-done with it for good, thank God!"

I said nothing in answer to this, for I saw that he only wanted to be left alone to go on talking, and, sure enough, he began again before a minute had passed.

"It's her brother that is setting himself against me," said he; "a bit of a man I could crumple up in my hand. That's why she doesn't want to be seen here in Paris in her own name. She's staying at the Scribe, and calls herself Mme. Grévin-she that is able to buy up the Rue de Rivoli and half the boulevards as well. Oh, but there'll be fun to come, man-fun to come."

"You had a pleasant evening, sir?" I asked at this point.

"Pleasant enough," replied he, "so far as it went. There was me and Mr. Ames dined at the Grand Café."

"Not at the Café de Paris, then, sir?" said I.

"No, not at the Café de Paris," said he; "it was her brother that kept her. He came unexpected from Trouville. But we'll have better luck, Hildebrand, on Friday, mark me. Oh, it was a great day entirely that sent me from Derbyshire to Paris."

With this he rolled into bed, and I put his light out. So far as I could make out, he had been to the Café de Paris, and had there heard that the lady was prevented from meeting him by her brother's arrival from Trouville. This sounded fair enough, yet what I wanted to know was how he came to dine with Mr. Ames and that laughing little bundle of goods, Mimi Marcel. But he never said a word about that, and next morning he was as silent as ever; nor did he open his lips to me until the following Friday, when at seven o'clock he left for the Hôtel Chatam, where the second appointment was made. What was my astonishment to see him back in an hour, and with him no other than Rudolphe Marcel, the brother of the little witch Mimi.

The two dined together in our own coffee-room, and then went over to play billiards with Jack Ames until twelve o'clock. It was two o'clock when Sir Nicolas went to bed, and he was so silent and snappish that I knew he'd been losing money. And what was worse, he never opened his lips to tell me why he had returned so unexpected from the Hôtel Chatam. That he had failed to meet the Baroness de Moncy I felt sure-yet how it had come about, or if he had received any letter, I never learned.

Now, it seemed to me, when I went to bed that night, that we had drifted into a very queer place. He had been spending money like water since the morning he received the present. 1 knew that there was precious little of his thousand pounds remaining. Of course, I'd had my bit —a matter of five hundred-out of what we took in Derbyshire; but money is money, and what I'd got was locked away safe enough. How he was going to get on in Paris without a guinea in his pocket, I didn't see; and this affair, upon which he reckoned, seemed as much in the clouds as ever. I had begun, in fact, to believe that he was running after a shadow altogether, and to that belief I should have stood if the next morning had not brought a turn as sudden as it was unlooked for; and one that made me fear not only for his purse, but for his life. It came about this way:

Sir Nicolas got out of bed at twelve o'clock, still rather short, and in what I call a "brandy-and-soda" temper. He dressed himself carelessly, and crossed over the road to the gardens of the Café" Rouge to get his *déjeûner*. Five minutes after he had gone there came a letter for him; a little bit of a note in a feminine hand, such as he had received often since the intrigue with the woman at Trouville began. I knew well that he'd make a fuss if he didn't get this *billet doux* at once, so I ran across the road to the café, just as I was, without hat or any thing. I found him sitting at a marble table, reading the morning's *Figaro;* but what should happen but that, just as I was beginning to talk to him, up stepped another man, a squat little party with a bushy black beard, and stood glaring at him over the table.

"Sare Nicolas Steele," says he, speaking funny-like and with a lot of French words in between that I couldn't make head or tail of—"do I spik to Sare Nicolas Steele?"

"You do," said my master, looking up at him over the paper.'

"Then I take leave to smack your face," says he; and, as I'm a man, he bent over and struck Sir Nicolas on the right cheek with his glove.

Now, if there's one thing more than another that you don't find an Irishman take quietly to, it's a blow on the face, be it ever so light. And Sir Nicolas wasn't different from other men. No sooner had the Frenchman touched him than he sprang up from his chair and rushed at him like a bull.

"Is it for smacking faces ye are?" says he, white with passion. "Then I'll take leave to join in with you!" and with that he sent the table and chairs flying, and I believe that he'd have killed him if some of us hadn't got in between the pair of them and held them apart.

As it was, he tore the Frenchman's coat from his collar to his hip, and the man's shirt looked like an old envelope. But he kept as quiet as ever; and when the landlord had come up, and there was a big crowd around the pair of them, he says quite calmly:

"Monsieur, my name is Eugene Grevin, and I am to be found at the Hôtel Scribe."

"Sir," says my master-and I never saw him look more dignified, "my friend shall call upon you at once."

Suddenly as the thing had been sprung upon me, the end of it was not less sudden. The Frenchman who called himself Grevin bowed to Sir Nicolas, Sir Nicolas bowed to him; and away they both went, the one to *fiacre* waiting for him, my master to his hotel. But I never saw him more excited, and the way he ordered me about was a thing to hear.

"Hildebrand," said he-and he couldn't rest in one place a minute, "I'll tear the throat of him. It's to him that we owe all this trouble and delay-him and no other."

"Then you know the party, sir?"

"Know him, the paltry scoundrel! and what would I be if I did not know him? He's the brother of the Baroness de Moncy. And it's to-morrow morning that I'll shoot him like a dog. Run now to Mr. Ames and tell him that he must come to me at once. I've need of him, and there's no time to lose."

Well, I left him drinking absinthe, and ran away to Mr. Ames' place just as fast as my legs could carry me. My head seemed so full of thinking that I was worse than one dazed, and all the houses danced before my eyes as I raced down the street.

"Good Lord!" said I, "that it should have come to this-him risking his life with pistols, and all for a woman who sent him her picture in a locket. And what if he's shot-what then, Bigg? You're not likely to tumble into a place like this for many a year; and you'd miss him, that you can't deny. Again, suppose he isn't shot, but kills the man? Where do you stand then? In Queer Street, I fancy, and the sooner you're out of Paris the better."

This is what I thought as I ran along to Mr. Ames'. If we shot our man, there'd be a hullaballoo which must be heard in London; and then who could tell where we might find ourselves? And what would the woman whom all the fuss was about do? She couldn't well stand by a man who had shot her own brother. Please God, we'll only wound him, thought I, and get away to Trouville while he's in the doctor's hands.

I found Mr. Ames dressed in a shabby old coat and standing before a big picture. He heard what I'd got to tell him before lie took his pipe from his mouth, and seemed to take it very serious.

"I'm coming along with you now," said he; and then he asked me a minute after, "Does he know any thing about pistols?"

"The devil a bit, sir," said I; "he can't abide 'em."

"And he's worse than a cow with a sword," said he next.

"Never had one in his hand that I know of, sir," I answered.

"Well," said he, "it's a bad job, and if he's alive this time to-morrow, he's a lucky man. Help me on with my coat, will you, now?"

I did as he asked me and we hurried back to the Hôtel de Lille. Sir Nicolas was pacing up and down the courtyard, and directly he caught sight of Mr. Ames, he began to talk to him.

"Jack," cried he, "ye've heard the news that I'm to go out with him?"

"Truth, I have; and a pretty mess you seem to have made of it."

"Mess, d'ye call it? Didn't he come here and strike me in the face? 'Tis lucky for him that I forgot to twist his neck."

"Then there's no question of apology?"

"Be hanged to your apology! Is it a coward ye think I am-me that would fight any man in France?"

"But what will Carlotta say?"

"What can she say, when it's for her that I'm meeting him? Wasn't it he who prevented her coming last night? Wasn't he the man who stopped her when she was to meet me at the Café de Paris? The devil take your apologies!"

"Then I'm to call on him?"

"Certainly ye are, and to have Rudolphe Marcel with you. There's no other that I know who would do it for me."

"He has the right of weapons," said Mr. Ames here.

"And don't I know it? What's it to me whether he's the right of weapons? Won't I kill him any way?"

Mr. Ames shook his head, and the two went off, walking arm and arm, to the house of Rudolphe Marcel. I saw them next at seven o'clock, when they were all dining at the Café Rouge, but Sir Nicolas never came home until midnight, and then he was more like a beaten child than a man.

"Hildebrand, Hildebrand," said he, "ye'll be burying me to-morrow, for sure. I'm to fight at dawn."

"Is that so, sir?" said I. "Well, sorry I am to hear it. There was never any good done yet in this world by blowing a man's brains out, and there won't be, I make sure. I wouldn't fight, if I were you, sir."

"Wouldn't fight-hark at him!" cried he. "Wouldn't fight-me that is the ninth baronet with forefathers big in history! Is it the chicken of the family I'm to be? What would she say of me if I refused him? No; by Heaven, I'll cut his throat."

"He hasn't chosen pistols, then, sir?" I asked next.

"Indeed, and he has."

I didn't want to hear this, for a duel with pistols looked like to be the death of one of them. But before I could say any thing he was rambling on again.

"If it pleases God that I'm killed," said he, "you will send the letter that I'm writing to the Baroness de Moncy at the Hôtel Chatam. My clothes you may keep, Hildebrand. Ye've been a good man to me, and I'll not forget to say so on paper."

"I do hope it won't be as bad as that, sir," said I.

"'Tis as God wishes," replied he, pious like, "and I don't forget I was born a Catholic, though I'm no credit to my religion."

"May I ask where you're to meet him, sir?" said I, trying to turn him from thinking of it.

"In the garden of a house at Vincennes, at six o'clock," he answered. "We'll be private there, and no police to interrupt. You'll not forget to wake me at five?"

I promised that I would not, and he sat down to his desk in his shirt-sleeves and wrote two letters. One he addressed to the Baroness de Moncy; the other was a character for me, and I couldn't have had a better one, not if I'd been the angel Gabriel. It made me queer to read it though, for all said and done I liked Nicky Steele; and there's few men in this world that ever I did like. But that wasn't the place to say so, and as the night went on, I had just as much as I could do to manage him. He'd been drinking cognac, you see, and there was a time, about four in the morning, when his courage left him, and he broke down like a woman.

"Hildebrand, Hildebrand," he wailed, lying on his bed, with his clothes on, "where will I be this time to-morrow? What's to become of me immortal soul? Is there no one that will bring a priest to me? Am I to die without a friend in the world-not a friend, by Heaven! —me that was born a Catholic?"

He went on like this for a good half hour; but I gave him some more drink, and about half-past four he began to doze. As for myself, I never closed my eyes, but sat there beside him, while the cold white dawn came creeping along the streets, and Paris bestirred herself to begin another day.

"Good Lord!" said I, looking down on his pale face, "to think that this time to-morrow your body may lie under the ground, and I may be loose on the road of life again, and all for the shadow of a woman who may mean nothing at all, and whom, like enough, you may never see again. Well, well! we've seen some queer times together, Sir Nicolas Steele, that we have; good times and bad times, days when we've not known where our dinner was coming from, and days when we could have taken a bath in the guineas. And now, it's come to this, that you're making yourself a pot-shot for a bit of a French chap I wouldn't soil my boots with. Did any one ever match that?"

All this was bothering me, I needn't tell, while I sat and watched him during the half-hour he slept. When I awoke him at last he seemed all the better for his doze, and was quite cool and collected, dressing himself up as smart as if he was going to Longchamps or Auteuil.

"Hildebrand," said he, "what bit of money I have is banked with Hébraie, as you know. It 'll serve to pay up here if any thing happens to me. All the little things are for you."

"Don't you think of that, sir," said I. "Just you keep your nerve, and shoot straight. I don't doubt you can hold a pistol as well as he can, if it comes to that."

"My fathers could, any way," he exclaimed, drinking up the coffee I'd brought him. "Is the cab at the door yet?"

"It's just driving up, sir," said I.

The cab, in which were Mr. Ames and Mr. Marcel, drove up while I talked to him; and they came bustling out and insisted on taking a liqueur together before leaving. I thought they both seemed in mighty good spirits, seeing what they were after; and Sir Nicolas thought so too.

"Well, boys," said he, "it's gay ye are, I must say. Did ye buy the pistols, Jack?"

"No need to do that," says Mr. Ames. "I brought a case of my own. And as for being gay, Nicky, you'll be shouting loud enough in half an hour, you mark my words."

"I have my doubts," says he, quite gloomy like; and then out they all went, while I climbed on the box, and we drove away toward the old Pont Bercy.

There weren't many people about the streets, for most of the working folk had gone already to business; but the air was crisp and sharp, like it is in early autumn, and the river was foaming up in little bits of waves, which did one good to see. By and by, we came out in the Rue des Buttes, and so crossed to the Cours de Vincennes, stopping at last before an ugly old house surrounded by trees, which were already losing their leaves. The next minute the gentlemen were on the pavement, and my master, pale, and a bit weak about the knees, as it seemed to me, went into the garden with them.

Until this time there had been no one to say me nay when I chose to follow the party. I had ridden on the box without asking any one, and I was going after Sir Nicolas into the garden, when an old white-haired footman tried to shut the gate in my face.

"Be hanged to your impudence!" said I, getting my foot in the way and giving him push for push; but it was a minute before I had the best of him, and while I was still pushing there was a shout of laughter came from the garden.

We found the party drawn up in a circle on the lawn. For some time I didn't know whether I was awake or dreaming, for what should I see but a capital breakfast spread under the trees, and twenty or thirty finely dressed women just holding their sides as though they would die of the spectacle. As for Sir Nicolas, he was standing before them with a look on his face as if he could strike them all dead where they sat. And talking to him was Jack Ames and a little, clean-shaven chap that I recognized as Louis Regnard.

"Permit me," says Jack Ames, bowing very low, while all the others went on with their laughing, "to present to you the Chevalier Eugene Grevin, *alias* M. Louis Regnard of the Theatre du Vaudeville. The Baroness de Moncy is yonder, resting under the trees. She is known sometimes as Juliette Vauloo, of the Théâtre de l'Opéra Comique."

"Hoaxed by — —!" says Sir Nicolas; and with this he fairly bolted out of the garden.

* * * * *

What did they make out of it? Well, reckoning the three dinners he stood Jack Ames while his head was full of the picture, and the dinner that he gave to Rudolphe and Mimi Marcel, and all the champagne that had been drunk during the week, it wasn't a bad thing; to say nothing of him playing billiards with Ames. The egg they sent him wasn't worth a sovereign. It was lined with lead.

And that reminds me. I heard of the real Baroness de Moncy the other day. She hadn't set foot out of Portugal for three years, and is a white-haired old woman, much troubled with rheumatics.

CHAPTER XI
MICHEL GREY IS MISSING

We remained in Paris for some weeks after the affair of the golden egg before there was any thing happened to us worth writing about. When the luck changed, if you call it luck, it did so sudden, and the strange adventure of which I now propose to speak was upon us all in a minute. I date it from the moment when I heard that Michel Grey, Sir Nicolas' American friend, was missing, and that not a soul in Paris could throw any light upon the circumstances of his disappearance. The man had vanished like a phantom, leaving no word, no message, no letter. The city had taken him from our sight. Whether he were alive or dead, in France or out of France, a willing absconder. or the victim of the assassin, neither friend nor enemy could tell. He had gone like the night, and had left us to face the problem as we might.

That it was a problem for us, and that we could not begin and end with his going, I never had a doubt. He had been seen about with Sir Nicolas for the best part of a month; my master's game with his sister, Dora Grey, was known to all the town about; there wasn't a servant in the hotel that didn't understand where the hate between the two men came from. And, to cap all, the man went away at the height of it, and we were left with the girl, and with all the talk that followed his disappearance.

Until this moment, I had looked upon the whole episode as a handsome turn of fortune. There were many weeks after the strange hoax of the golden egg when my master never put his nose outside the Hôtel de Lille. In all the years I've known him, I can never remember such an upset as that business was to his health and to his energy. He seemed just like one stupefied, with no taste for work and no taste for play. The little money that he possessed dribbled away pound by pound, until I had to find what was wanted even for his daily living. He no longer earned any thing at the billiard table; he scarce read the newspapers. There were days when he never got up from his bed; days when he did not open his lips to man or woman. And I do believe that he was never so low, or in such a queer way, as upon the evening that brought him face to face with Dora Grey, and gave a turn to his life which he was to feel for many years.

She came to the hotel quite sudden-an auburn- haired, blue-eyed little thing, with the fairest skin woman ever had, and a way with her which was wonderful to see. The name down in the visitors' book was "Dora Grey of Boston," and just above it, I saw written, "Michel Grey, artist." But I didn't mark the man until the following morning, though Sir Nicolas, who had gone down into the garden that night, the first time for many weeks, was as full of the pair of them as he could be.

"Hildebrand," says he, "there's an American couple below which is worth the knowing. She's an artist from Boston, and she's come to the schools. It's the Greys, the railway people, they are; and rolling in the money. Did ye hear a fair-haired girl laughing at the top of her voice in the garden? Well, that's the one I mean. Faith, 'tis speaking manners these Americans have, for sure. She'd told me her history before we'd done the soup."

"Is she staying long, sir?" I asked.

"Three months certain, and likely longer. She's come here to be near the painting. It was her brother that sat opposite Jack Ames to-night. A white-faced man; with a liver, I'll wager. I'll know him better this time to-morrow."

It was extraordinary, I must say, to see how a little thing like this drew him out of himself. While he'd gone down to dinner telling me that I should find his body in the Morgue before the month was out, he came to bed all cheerful like a boy, and next morning he took an hour to dress himself. I saw him sitting down with the Americans to *déjeúner;* and after dinner he was three hours with the brother over at the billiard-room at the Cafe Rouge. Then I knew that the business had begun, and that luck had lifted us out of the groove again.

"They're a queer couple altogether, Hildebrand," says Sir Nicolas, when I took him his coffee next morning. "Bedad! the man puzzles me. He's as mean of the money as a Scotchman out of

Montrose. There was three hours we were playing last night, and not a sovereign changed hands."

"You won't pay many bills out of that, sir," says I.

"And don't I know it? Isn't it the girl I'm thinking of? They're the railway people, I'd be tellin' you-the Greys of Boston. That was a lucky day which sent them to the Hôtel de Lille; and for three months, too! You can do much with a woman in three months, Hildebrand."

"That you can, sir, if she's willing."

"Oh, she'll be willing enough by and by. There's no sugar for an American tongue like a title to roll over it. I was the man of the party before I'd known her an hour. She's just the sweetest bit of a brogue you ever heard, and her father's worth five million dollars. Get me my light frock-coat, will you now? I'm to drive her to St. Cloud this very morning."

Well, he went off with her sure enough, the pair of them dressed up until you might have picked them out of a thousand. When he was gone, and the place was put a bit straight, I strolled over to the Café Rouge to get my lunch and read the English papers. Paris was beginning to be full again then, for we were almost through the autumn, and the gardens were cold at nights. But you could find the folks you wanted any time from midday until four, and no sooner was I in the place than I saw Michel Grey, the brother of the little American woman Sir Nicolas had just driven to St. Cloud. He was sit- ting at a table, and there was a bottle of hock before him.

"Halloa, my man!" cried he, as I passed him, and he didn't speak a bit like an American; "I'd like half a dozen words with you, if you don't mind."

"With the greatest pleasure in life, sir," I replied, thinking, at the same time, what a peculiar looking gentleman he was.

"Is it long since you left Dublin?" asks he, quite calm like, and pretending to see nothing of the start I gave.

"Would that be any business of yours?" I said, sharp and short, and looking at him in a way he couldn't mistake.

"Certainly it would be," says he. "A cousin of mine knew a Sir Nicolas Steele in Dublin three years ago, and I was wondering if it was the same."

"Then you should have asked my guv'nor," says I, while my heart began to jump so that I could hardly hold my hand still.

"Oh, no offence!" cries he, and with that he slipped a five-franc piece into my hand.

"You've been in Paris long?" he asks.

"A month or more," says I, thinking where I could have him.

"Are you going back to England soon?"

"We are going back at the end of November. Sir Nicolas has engagements in London that month."

"Oh! then you *are* going back."

"Why, what would we be doing all the winter here in Paris?"

He seemed to think a while over this, taking a drink of the hock and rolling his bleary eyes as though he was looking for some one in the garden. Presently he said;

"Do you like the situation you're in?"

"Oh!" said I, "it's much the same as other situations. Here to-day and gone to-morrow."

"Then you travel a good deal?"

"That's so-but travel or no travel, it's all the same to me."

"Your master seems a pleasant sort of gentleman?"

"I should call him that."

"He's a baronet or something, isn't he?"

"Exactly; he's Sir Nicolas Steele of Castle Rath, County Kerry."

"A generous man, I should say."

I looked at him straight, for I'd read him up by this time.

"It's a cold morning for talking in the open air, sir," says I, and with that I turned on my heel and left him.

Now, though I had taken it coolly enough, a duller head than mine could have seen through the man's talk.

"What's in the wind is this," said I to myself when I got back to the hotel, "you've heard some gossip, my fine gentleman, and you want to get to the bottom of it. If it's true that a cousin of yours knew Sir Nicolas Steele in Dublin three years ago, then you'll write to him, and what you'll learn won't keep your sister at the Hôtel de Lille. Maybe that cousin is in Europe; more probably he's in America, which gives us a month. Any way, it's you that we've got to play, and the sooner we begin the better."

This was my thought, and yet, simple as it seemed, there was something happened later in the day which gave a new turn altogether to it. I'd been bothering my head with the matter all afternoon, making nothing new of it outside the fact that the danger signal had been rung, so to speak, when what would happen but that, just before seven o'clock, I met the man again, face to face, in the corridor of the hotel, and the sight of him fairly took my breath away. I shouldn't have called him a healthy person any time, but now his eyes were sunken away something dreadful to see-while his cheeks were hollow like the cheeks of one just got up from a fever bed. White as his face had been in the morning, the color of it in the afternoon was like a bit of plaster of Paris. And what was more than this was the way he walked, feeling his road with his hands, like a blind man, and staring before him as though he was frightened that every step he took might land him on nothing.

Never have I seen the muscles of a man's mouth twitch so much, or a man's fingers look so like claws. If he had been stark raving mad he could not have given me a greater shock; and I stood there, feeling like a child that has seen something horrible on the stairs and does not know whether to go forward or to go back.

There was a minute when, seeing him clutch hold of the banister and fix his dreadful eyes on me, I thought he was going to strike me. He half raised his right arm, but let it drop quickly again and began to mumble something that I could not hear. His speech was thick like that of a drunken man, and vet I could have sworn that drink was not the matter with him. Quite otherwise, he appeared to be in great pain; and when he got his words out at last, they came with gasps like the words of a man suffering.

"Where's your shoddy baronet?" he asked.

"What's that?" said I.

"Your Nicolas Steele, card-sharper and thief?" he went on, and this took me more aback than if he'd hit me.

"Look here," said I, "you're a bold man, but if you don't want to be horsewhipped out of this hotel, don't say that twice."

"Then you mean to say that he isn't?"

"A hundred times! A more honorable gentleman doesn't breathe in Paris, and if it wasn't for the state you are in, young man, I'd let you know it too."

This silenced him a bit. He stood rocking on his heels for a minute or more, and then, muttering something between his teeth which I could not make out, he continued his march up the stairs. A quarter of an hour later, Sir Nicolas himself drove up with the young American, and he hadn't been in the hotel two minutes before I'd told him what had passed and what I'd seen. Strange to say, he took it as calm as a man hearing of the weather.

"The fellow's a lunatic-that's what he is," he cried, while he began to dress for the opera; "she's told me his history, coming home. He's a drug- drinker, and what he remembers to-day he'll know nothing of to-morrow, or perhaps for a month or more. Ye needn't mind him no more than a toy-pistol. I have her word for it, and that's good enough for me."

"Then his cousin wasn't in Dublin three years ago?" asked I.

"Indeed and he was, and that's the humor of it. He left before my affair, d'ye see, and if they write him, it's a pretty tale of me he'll be telling. Bedad! I couldn't have wished it better if me own hands had the planning of it."

"I'm glad to hear that, sir," said I, "so long as the young lady doesn't listen."

"Listen! Not she. 'Tis easy for the ears to be shut when the heart is open. Sure, won't I be marrying her within the month? She's American, you must remember, and tied to nobody's apron-strings. Oh, it was a famous day that kept us at the Hôtel de Lille!"

He said this quite unconcerned, and not a bit ready to argue the point out with me. It was all very well for him to glide over it in that easy way, but what I wanted to know was, where had Michel Grey first heard talk about us? That the gossip was new to him was evident from the fact that he played billiards with my master the very first night he came to Paris. What chatter he had heard was heard between supper that evening and breakfast two days after. And this was what troubled me, even in the face of Sir Nicolas' tale about him taking drugs and forget- ting. "There's danger moving," I thought, "and if you're married within the month, Nicky, I'm a Chinaman."

This is how the thing looked to me, then and for days after. While, on the one hand, Michel Grey talked no more, either to me or to Sir Nicolas, of his suspicions, on the other hand, I could see that he would have no truck with us, and was doing his best to make his sister think as he did. That he did not succeed in this is to be set down to many things, but above all to the fact that for days together he would hang about the hotel like a man without a mind; and was, as all the world could see, tottering fast to his grave. What drug he drank, or where he learned the habit, no man could say, but a more pitiable spectacle than he made, looking for all the world like a blind thing come out of a coffin, I hope never to see. Luckily for us, there was no affection lost between him and Miss Dora. Talk as he might, the day was rare when she did not plan some excursion with my master. They spent hours together out at Fontainebleau or Versailles-were half their leisure time at the picture-galleries, the other half at the *cafés* and theatres. I saw them walking arm-in-arm in the gardens, I saw him kiss her when she went to her painting in the morning, I saw him kiss her when she came home again to *déjeúner*, and I began to think that after all he was right and I was wrong. Then, all of a sudden, the trouble came, and we woke up from our dream.

Michel Grey had disappeared. For the first time since we had been at the hotel, he had exchanged words with my master over the dinner- table. It did not come to blows, but the hands of the people around alone kept the two men apart, and Sir Nicolas was heard by twenty folks to say that he'd beat the life out of the American with his hunting-crop. That night and the next Michel Grey did not sleep in his bed at the Hôtel de Lille. At ten o'clock two mornings later his sister Dora was knocking at my master's door, wanting to know what he had done with him.

I can see her now, with her pretty hair streaming down her back, and her face so flushed that she might have been rubbing her cheeks with a glove. Many women would have thought nothing of a man going off like that; but the quarrel stuck in her head, I suppose, and she was as scared as a rabbit. When

Sir Nicolas came out to her, she was no longer gentle with him as she had been before this, but stamped her foot and spoke angrily, with quick, biting words.

"Well," she cried, "where is he? You know, of course?"

"As God is my witness, I know nothing," said he.

"But you were with him last-you were the last to speak to him."

"Indeed, and I was; and when he'd done with me, he went straight to his bedroom. Dora, it's not lies that I'd tell you at such a time."

"Then where is he? what has happened to him? what shall I tell my father? Oh, they love him at home; indeed they do!"

She began to cry at this, and my master took her hand.

“You poor little thing!” said he, drawing her head down upon his shoulder. “Would I harm him, whatever he was-and your brother, too? Don’t ye see, child, that he’s just gone off in a bit of a huff, and will be back before your tears are dry. Ye’ll be the first to laugh when he walks in here.”

“He is not the man to do that,” said she, though she was no longer angry. “I am sure of it. I dreamed of him all night. He is dead, Nicolas.”

Now what should Sir Nicolas do when she said this but give her a great kiss, and burst out laughing.

“Dead!” said he, “then I’m thinking we should get ready for the waking, and ask him to crack the first bottle. Bedad! he’s as dead as I am, little woman, and don’t you think any such thing. Whatever put that into your head?”

“I could not tell you,” said she. “We do not think these things-we know them.”

At this he set off laughing again, and did his best to cheer her up-though it was poor work he made of it at the best. By and by, when he had seen a nice little breakfast sent up to her rooms, he came to me, and I knew then that he took it worse than I thought he would.

“Well,” says he, “the fool’s gone, right enough. There’s no word or sign yet. I’ll begin to think by and by that harm has come to him.”

“In that case, sir,” said I, “it’s pity that what was said two nights ago couldn’t wait.”

“How do you mean?” he asked.

“Why-it’s no good disguising it-you threatened to murder him.”

“Good God! Would they think that?”

“There’s some that might.”

He stood stock still when I had said this, and his face was very white.

“It’s luck to make one gnash the teeth,” said he presently. “I’d have married her within the week!”

“There’s no reason why you shouldn’t now, sir,” said I, “always supposing that it’s well with him. But there are things to do.”

“You think so?”

”Certainly; and if it was me that was concerned,

I’d be up at the police-station before the clock struck again.”

“Do you believe they would find him?”

“They might, or they might not; but it would be cover for you.”

“I’ll do that,” said he shortly. “Is there any thing else?”

“One thing,” said I. “This young fellow has a father in America. If three days pass and we hear nothing of him, send a cable out to Boston, and advise that a reward be offered—a big one, say ten thousand dollars. Meanwhile, offer a reward of two thousand francs yourself.”

“But I’d have to pay. What’s the sense in that?”

“Sir,” I said, “if Mr. Grey of Boston will offer a reward of ten thousand dollars for the recovery of his son, there is one man who will find him.”

“And who is that, pray?”

“Myself.”

He looked at me with blank amazement. Then he said quite simply;

“Ye’re a clever man. I’d be sorry for the day when we parted.”

“But we must part, sir,” said I.

“’Tis no time for nonsense, sure,” said he.

“And it’s no nonsense I mean, sir. If I’m to find this man and to claim this reward, the work must be done away from here.”

“Where would it be done, then?”

“From the house in the Rue Dupin, where we lived two years ago.”

He thought over it a little while, and then he said;

“It’s the devil of a head ye’ve got. How did you come to think of it?”

“Common-sense taught me,” said I. “There’s many a worse friend, sir.”

CHAPTER XII
AT THE MAISON D'OR

A week after this talk I left the Hôtel de Lille and took a lodging in a little house in the Rue Dupin. It was the first time in my life that ever I'd set to work to hunt a man, and I knew at the beginning of it that I had a stiff job before me. Notwithstanding the light way we had taken Michel Grey's disappearance, seven days had passed and no living soul had heard a word of him. He had gone like a light in a wind, and had left neither letter nor message. While some were bold enough to say that Nicolas Steele could have told the tale, most people were deceived by the pains my master took to trace the missing man. None the less, it was not hidden from me that the police were watching him, and that any minute he might be face to face with the greatest peril of his life.

My object in moving from the hotel to the Rue Dupin was a simple one. Jonathan Grey, the father of the missing man, had walked into the trap we had set for him like a child into a sweetstuff-shop. His answer to his daughter's cable was immediate. "Offer the reward," he said, and we had offered it. That is to say, we had printed a thousand bills and had burned them.

"Once get those bills about Paris," said I to Sir Nicolas, "and your man's here in a couple of hours. That don't suit us when ten thousand dollars are at stake-not by a long way. If Michel Grey is to be found at all, I'm going to find him, and to bank half the reward in my name. The other half is yours by every right."

"I've nothing to say against that," exclaimed he; "it's what I was thinking of myself. But ye don't tell me who's to claim the money, and all the world knowing that you're my servant. You don't forget that we're dealing with Yankees?"

"I forget nothing, sir," said I, "and that's what takes me to the Rue Dupin. The man who will claim the reward is my friend, Jim Pascoe — —"

"What! Jim Pascoe, the tout?"

"No other. If there's any thing in Paris that's new to him, I should be glad to hear of it. He'll do the job for a hundred pounds, and gladly."

"Ye don't fear to trust him?"

"Fear!" replied I, "why, I know enough about Jim Pascoe to buy a dozen men."

This was a true word, and half an hour after it was spoken I was seated with Jim in the little bit of a cabin in the Rue Dupin, where I told him the tale. Jim was a man who got his living the best way he could, but chiefly at Auteuil and Longchamps, and in being father-in-law to the English mugs who want to "do" Paris. If any one could say what bad become of Michel Grey, he was the man; and I'd hardly got the words out of my lips when he jumped down my throat with his theory.

"Bigg," says he, "your man's in a drug-den —and what's more, he's in a private drug-den. It's a wonder his people haven't had any note for money before this-that is, if Grey hasn't a banking account of his own in Paris."

"I don't follow you there," says I. "What do you mean by a private drug-den?"

"Why, a place where they dose 'em and bleed 'em at the same time. Such shops are cheap this way. They trap a man with cash, aud make it pleasant for him so long as his money lasts, then they knock him on the head or leave him to skip the golden gutter. You couldn't have named a worse job. I doubt that you'll ever set eyes on Grey again, if you live to be a hundred."

This was a facer! I'd thought all along that the American was laid by the heels in some opium-shop, but that we should have any difficulty in getting him out was a fact that never entered my head.

"Then you don't take the thing on, Jim?" said I.

"Oh, I'm not saying that!" cried he; "but it's worth more than a hundred. I'm like to have my head cracked before I'm out of it."

"I'll make it two hundred and fifty," said I, "and not a penny more."

"You're on," says he. " And now for a word about the chap's duds. What was he wearing when last you saw him?"

I gave him a full account of Michel Grey and his clothes, and he went away. Twenty-four hours after I got a line from him:

> "Come up to the Rue de la Loire. I have found your man."

You may imagine that I didn't lose much time in doing as he asked me. While I couldn't really believe that the thing was to end in the simple way his letter made out, none the less the fact that we stood a good chance now of putting our hands on the ten thousand dollars came home to me.

"Bigg," said I, "you'll be set up for a twelve-month, and Sir Nicolas 'll be off to New York to marry a Yankee-that is, if he doesn't close on that pretty bit of goods up at the Hôtel de Lille. Was there ever such a town?"

I found Jim sitting on a dirty bed in a dirty little house near the boulevard end of the street he had named. He didn't look at all hopeful, as I expected he would, and the cigar that he held in his hand had gone out.

Well," says he, "you got my letter?"

"Why should I be here if I hadn't?" says I.

"Ah, true!" he went on; "and I may as well tell you at once—I believe your man's at the Maison d'Or, up in Montmartre."

"How did you find that out?" I asked.

"I traced him by his stick," said he; "an orange-wood cane, with a globe of silver and a little map of the world on the top of it. Is that it?"

"The same," cried I.

"And he wore a hat of black felt, large beyond usual?"

"He did that."

"Then he's at the Maison d'Or; and how we're to get him out, God knows."

"Why, what's the difficulty?"

"I don't like the house," says he, shifting his eyes curiously.

"But what's the matter with it?"

"Oh, there's nothing the matter with it-except that a good many who go in never come out again. I've no fancy for that myself."

"Jim," says I, "you haven't got the heart of a rabbit. What nonsense you're talking! Take me up to the shop, and let me have a look at it."

"I was going to suggest that," says he. "It 'll be dark in an hour, and no one to tread on our heels. I know the woman who keeps the *cabaret* at the back of the place. It was from the top of a shed in her garden that I looked down into the lower rooms."

"Why not knock at the door at once and have done with it?" says I.

"It would be worth more than your life or mine to do that," cried he. "All the neighborhood knows it. There's not a man that would venture in."

"Then what makes you think that this Grey is there?"

"He was two days at an opium-den in the Rue d'Oran, which is not a stone's- throw off, and was last seen at the *cabaret* I speak of. He was then with the man who runs the Maison d'Or. Folks knew him from my description of his hat and stick. I guessed at once that I should hear of him in a drug-shop. That's what took me to the Rue d'Oran."

"You're friends with the woman who runs this beer-shop, did you say?"

"The best possible, though I wouldn't walk with her in the Bois-not for choice, leastwise."

"Then let's get up there at once. If Grey is in the shop, the closer the eye we keep on it the better."

He assented to this, and we went off together in a closed cab. It was then almost full dusk, and threatening for a wet night. In fact, we hadn't got to the top of the Rue du Faubourg when the rain began to pelt down in earnest, the people scuttling into the *cafés*, and the water flooding the gutters. When at last our rickety old cab began to lumber up the slopes of Montmartre, the lamps in the streets were dancing before a stiff west wind, and the sky above us was black as ink. Where we'd got to, I couldn't for the life of me tell; but by and by Jim stopped the driver before a third-rate drinking-den, and we stepped out in a dirty street, where the mud was almost up to our ankles.

"This is the place," said he; while it rained so fast that the water began to run off his hat. "Jam your tile over your eyes, and follow me. You will want a twenty-franc piece to shut the old woman's mouth. After that, it's easy."

He led the way into a bit of a bar, where four or five shabby customers were drinking beer and talking to women who matched them down to the ankles. But we weren't there more than a moment, for after a word in French lingo to the chap who served the drink, we passed on to a small parlor which overlooked a bit of a yard. Here a squat little woman, who didn't appear to have washed her face for a fortnight, was in talk with a girl who had a guitar in her hand—a poor, bespangled, squalid-looking wretch, who made her living, I don't doubt, by capering about before the scum in the bar. They left off when we came in, and then Jim fell to parleying with the woman, and a fine noise they made of it.

"She thinks you're a nark," said he to me in the middle of it. "Give us the twenty-franc piece, and see if that will cool her."

I handed him over the money, and they got to work again. This time the woman took it different; and when I'd whispered to him to promise her twenty francs more when we were through, she left off talking of a sudden, and led us down some dark stairs to a stinking kitchen where I wouldn't have housed a dog. Two minutes after we were out in the back yard, and she had left us.

"Now," said Jim, "we're the better for wanting her, though she's a wonderful woman when you take her right. The fact is, she's just as crazy as the others about that house yonder, and is half afeared of having any thing to do with us. But she's lent me the steps, and that's all I care a crack about."

It was raining cats and dogs now, and bitter cold, but we were both excited by what we'd come to do, and didn't feel it more than the touch of a feather. For my part, I'd thought little of the danger up to that time, but when I stood out in that dark yard and looked up to the black shape of a windowless and prison-like house, I must say that I got a shiver through me.

"Jim," said I, "two's not many for a job like this. Did you bring your pistol?"

"I did so," he whispered. "You don't find me going far without it in Paris. Will you go first, or shall I?"

"You go," said I, "since you know the way. I'm on your heels-though what you're to see through that wall I'd like to learn."

"There's windows on the lower story," cried he; "but keep your mouth shut, and tread light."

Saying this, he went up the steps, and I followed him. I have made it plain, I think, that the *cabaret* or beer-shop, or whatever you like to call it, stood back to back with the house we'd come to enquire about. There was only a yard and a high wall between them; but at the end of this yard, and jammed up against the wall, was a shed for lumber, so built that when you set the steps on its roof you could put your fingers on the top of the bricks above and haul yourself up. It didn't take Jim and I a minute to do this; and once astride the wall, we had our first view of the Maison d'Or.

I must say, and I always have said, that there was something uncanny in the very look of that house. Its heavy, blackened shape seemed to rise up like the shape of a dead-house or a prison. Many of its lower windows were heavily barred with iron bars. The paved yard around it was reeking with filth and rubbish. No sound, no light came out of it. It was just a great mass of brick-work looming up in the darkness, and I could understand easily enough how all the wild tales about it had come to be told. Sitting there, astride on the wall, and peering at such casements as faced the back of the cabaret, I should not have been a bit surprised if I'd have seen some inhuman thing stalking the yard below me. My heart was in my mouth-my nerves twitched like a woman's. And Jim was not a whit better.

"Do you make any thing of it?" he whispered, after we'd been on the wall a minute or two.

"The devil a bit!" said I.

"It ain't exactly a palace of varieties, is it?" he continued presently; "but Grey's in there, right enough. It was through that mite of a window on your left that I got a sight of the place last night. There was a light there then. I don't fancy we'll do much to-night."

"Nor me neither," said I, for I was right down scared, and that's the fact of it.

"Shall we try again to-morrow night?" said he, and I could see he was in a hurry to be off.

"We might as well, for all the good we're doing," said I; and with that I turned to put my foot on the steps again. A moment later I saw a thing which fairly took my breath away.

The window which was dark had suddenly become light. A man with a lamp in his hand passed it, and following him with quick steps was no other than my master, Nicolas Steele.

"Good God!" said I, half aloud, in spite of myself. "What are you doing in there?" and then, as I'm a man, I began to tremble. But Jim had already turned on me.

"Bigg," cried he, "you're playing me double! What's Nicolas Steele doing in there?"

"Ask me another," said I. "It's a thing I can't tell you."

"But I can!" said he, and he was angry too. "He's gone to get Grey out and claim the money."

"Jim, shut your mouth," said I, "and don't make him out the biggest fool alive!"

"You're playing me false!" cried he, raising his voice sillily.

"No such thing," said I. "And look here—I'll prove it. I'm going in after him."

"You are!" exclaimed he. "Then I'll say 'Good-evening' to you."

"Jim," said I, "don't you see it may be a matter of life or death with him? Help me in this, and I'll give you another hundred."

"Help you-how can I help you?"

"I'll tell you in a word. Run into the beer-shop there, and bring all the men you can find to these leads. Promise them twenty francs apiece to shout when I call to them. They'll do it quick enough if you say the police are with us on the other side."

"But you, yourself?"

"I'm going to throw these steps across the gap there, and force that window. After that, I'm trusting to bluff."

"You take your life in your hands," said he.

"Don't you trouble about that. You get the men. Quick's the word for this job."

He didn't wait for any more, but tumbled down to the shed again, and when I had waited five minutes and had seen him come out with half a dozen loafers at his tail, I dragged the steps up to the top of the wall, and then used them to bridge the gap which lay between the little window and myself. Luckily, the sill was old and broad; and though the window itself was not more than three feet square, it was unbarred. At any other time, I might have been a bit giddy clambering across that gap, for there was a drop of near twenty feet below me, but there were too many things running in my head to let me think of that, and half a minute hadn't gone before I had forced the window with my pocket-knife and dropped into a narrow passage on the second floor of the Maison d'Or.

Ten seconds, perhaps, I stood to assure myself that I was all right. Then I drew my revolver, and putting it to the full cock, I began to look about me. It was plain in a minute that I was in a passage with doors opening down one side of it. The glimmer of a light showed at the far end; but elsewhere it was all dark, and, what was more, strangely silent. The air itself was heavy, like the air of a bakehouse. I had to gasp for my breath; there was a choking sensation in my throat which nearly made me faint. Stinking fumes, like the fumes of stale opium, filled all the corridor and seemed to exude from the rooms. I staggered under the power of them, and had to bite my lips to prevent myself coughing.

So far as furniture went, there was little that I could see in the passage. A heavy carpet was soft to the feet, and thick curtains, made of some soft stuff, were hung over the openings to the doors. Yet what appeared more curious than any thing was the queer silence in the place. While I stood there, half choking for my breath, and half hidden behind one of the thickest of the curtains, I didn't hear so much as a creak of a door or the fall of a foot. The house might have been a dead-house with spectres for tenants.

You may ask me, fairly enough, what I had meant to do when I crossed the gap and forced my way into this queer place. I can only answer that I know no more than the dead. What I did was done on impulse. It was only when I stood in the passage, and heard my heart beating like a machine, that I began to think what a fool I had made of myself. And I must have stood there five minutes, afraid to go on, afraid to go back, when all of a sudden some one else decided for me. A door opened not two yards away, and out walked Sir Nicolas Steele and a little Frenchman. They were talking together angrily; and they went straight down the passage and turned the corner where the light was.

Though the door of the room from which they had come had only been open for a moment, I had seen a sight strange enough to have upset a stronger man than me. In a great Eastern-like room, all lit up with queer-colored lanterns, and having a fountain of water splashing in the middle of it, some twenty men were lying on little beds. Most of them looked to me to be dead with sleep, but one was raving, with his face buried in his pillow, while another seemed to be crawling on his hands and knees to the water which bubbled under the dome. The door was only open a second, as I say, but the view behind it gave me a shiver, and the shiver was still on me when, treading like a cat, I followed my master down the passage and came within a yard of him at the corner of it.

I was now near by the light, but curtains, hung crosswise in the passage, hid me well enough. I could see from my place that Sir Nicolas was arguing with the Frenchman at the top of a little flight of iron stairs. When they had talked for about a minute the Frenchman pointed to a door at the bottom of the flight, and my master made a step downward as though to reach the door. But his foot was hardly on the stairs when something happened which sent me as stiff as a corpse, and drew from me a cry which might have come from a madman. The stairs which I had seen a minute before I saw no longer. They had swung away under my master's touch, and with another cry joined to mine, he went headlong down to the floor below.

What happened in the next few minutes I can hardly tell. I remember, perfectly, that the Frenchman stood for a minute glaring at me, and hissing words between his teeth. Then he pressed a knob on the railings at his side, and the staircase swung back into its place.

So astonished was I to see such a thing that I never thought of the danger to myself. All that I could do was to stand and stare like one bewitched, and I don't believe that I had moved foot or hand when the man closed with me, and we went rolling over and over on the floor together. Strong man as I am, I don't think that I have ever been so near to death as I was that night. Now up, now down, with the cold sweat on my forehead, and the devil's fingers tearing the flesh out of my neck, I halloed to Jim to help me, and fought the Frenchman through. When I had done with him at last, I was covered with blood-but it was Jim who pulled me to my feet, Jim and Michel Grey, who stood, half-dressed, in the passage.

The noise and din which followed this business is not to be described by any man like me. While I stood half-blinded, and with roaring sounds in my ears, gendarmes seemed to be filling all the Maison d'Or. But I had my wits about me, and I turned to Jim.

"Get Grey out," said I, "and take him in a cab to the Hôtel de Lille. We'll lose the reward if you don't. Tell him his father's there. I'm after Sir Nicolas."

"Is he here?" he asked, as he went to do what I bid him.

"God knows whether he is alive or dead," said I; and with that I called to the gendarmes and showed them the swinging staircase.

Five minutes after, we were down in a filthy cellar, standing over the motionless body of my master. But his groans told us that he lived, and when lights were brought we knew to what he owed his life. He had fallen on the dead body of another victim of the Maison d'Or.

* * * * *

Well, that's the story of the phantom staircase, though there are some things left you might like to know. How did Sir Nicolas Steele come to the shop, for instance? Why, it appeared that after they had got Grey in the house-which was one of the largest and one of the lowest dens in Paris-they'd kept him drunk with the drug, in the hope that he'd add more money to what they'd robbed him of. On the day Jim and I set out for the cabaret, Grey had sent a messenger down to the Hôtel de Lille to get some of his traps and things. Sir Nicolas came across this messenger, and bribed the whole tale out of him. After that, he didn't want to lose a minute tracing the man, and he went straight off to Montmartre, leaving word at the police-station of what he'd done. The police had long been watching the shop, and when they heard that an Englishman was going there, they sent gendarmes after him-and lucky, too, or this story would not have been written.

How Sir Nicolas was so foolish as to stand between us and the chance of a reward, I only learned when he came to consciousness, nine days after we took him off the dead man's body in the cellar.

"And didn't I begin to be afraid of the whole thing?" said he. "Sure, the police were watching me night and day just as if I was a murderer. Reward or no reward, I was glad to have done with it."

And that was the truth, though old Jonathan Grey, after he'd heard what the police had to say, paid over every shilling of the money he'd promised, and gave me a hundred more for myself. But he was out of Paris while my master lay unconscious, and though Dora Grey cried enough for three, her studies in painting closed on the spot.

The Maison d'Or is pulled down now. I've no doubt myself that many a good man walked down those steps to his death. A more cunning trap you couldn't find. The whole flight of steps swung on a hinge at the top, and was caught at the bottom by a bit of the landing which projected, and which a spring held in its place. And it was a better weapon for a rogue than any knife or pistol.

CHAPTER XIII
THE GREAT WHITE DIAMOND

Nicky did not forget his visit to the Maison d'Or for a very long time. He would have remembered it longer if I had not found something else for him to think about, and set him going on a job which I shall always look back upon as the boldest we ever undertook in all our years together. It was this job which carried me for the first time in my life to the city of Vienna; and I can recollect, as if it happened yesterday, the night when we arrived there, and played the first card in as big an undertaking as two men ever put their hands to.

They were just beginning to light up the shops in the Graben and the Kohlmarkt, when we found the place we wanted, and stood for a minute, bitter cold as it was, to look at all the pretty things in the windows. Such passers-by as we saw were mostly business folk hurrying home to their dinners. Trade was done for the day, and done early, as it always is in that queen of cities, Vienna. Yet Sir Nicolas and I were at the very start of the greatest venture of our lives.

It seemed odd to me, I will say, to stand there in that old-town street of pretty shops and pretty women, and to remember what an errand bad brought us from Paris to the far end of Europe. Nor, I make sure, did it come home any the less to Sir Nicolas Steele. He had been crying out, ever since we left the Northern station, that failure was dogging our footsteps. He had stopped already before the shops of three jewellers and had refused to go in. And now, when we had found Lobmeyr's, and had only to turn the handle of their door to set the thing in train, what must he do but begin to laugh like a schoolboy and declare he couldn't go on with it.

"Sure," said he, rocking on his heels before the great glass window, "'tis a queer errand, I'm thinking."

"If that's your idea, sir," said I, "it's a pity you didn't stop in Paris. We shall do no good gaping here like schoolboys."

"But what if they won't take my references?"

"Ask me that when they have declined them. Count Horowitz's letter should be good enough for any shopkeeper in Vienna."

"Faith, ye're right there! but you forget that they might wire to Rome to confirm it."

"And if they do, what then? How's he to know that you're calling yourself Count Laon, or that the real Count Laon is in Paris? He'll think he's come here sudden and wants a word."

"That's true," said he, becoming very serious and even a bit nervous, I thought—"that's true; and I may very well pass for a Frenchman. Would you be asking for the big diamonds at once?"

"Certainly I would, sir. There's nothing to be got by beating about the bush. Say it's a commission from London. That and your letter will be enough."

He heard me out, still hesitating.

"Don't you think we'd do better in the morning?" he whispered, with his hand on the door of the shop.

"Sir," said I, for I knew the time had come when it must be neck or nothing, "if you want to turn your back on ten thousand pounds, which you can have almost for the asking, my advice is that you take the next train back to Paris."

"Well," said he, turning the handle suddenly, "you're a bold man, and ye've got the devil's own head on your shoulders. Bedad! I'll go through with it, if it lands the pair of us in the town jail before the morning."

He said this, and the next moment we were in the shop. It was a smallish place, so to speak, for such a man as Lobmeyr, who's talked of as the biggest diamond merchant in Vienna; but you could see with half an eye that there was valuable stuff under the glass cases, and there was the suggestion of solidity in the very chairs. I hadn't been in the house ten seconds when I marked a couple of rubies which would have fetched a thousand pounds apiece in Bond Street, and as for diamonds, they were there as big as nuts, and of a quality which made the whole shop a perfect sparkle of dazzling lights. I saw at once that we should get what we wanted;

and I waited for. Sir Nicolas to speak to the bald-headed little man, who bowed and scraped directly he set eyes on us, and did nothing else for the next ten minutes.

My master spoke in French, and though there were things that I could not follow, I had not been in Paris all those months without getting a bit of a grip on the lingo. I was anxious enough, you may understand, that Sir Nicolas should carry himself with confidence; but I must say that directly he had passed the shop-door he played the game like a man.

"Good-evening," said he. "I am the Comte de Laon, and have an introduction to Herr Lobmeyr from my friend Count Horowitz. Is it possible to see him to-night?"

"Perfectly," replied the other; "he is at this moment in his office."

"Then pray present this note to him, and say that the Comte de Laon and Sir Nicolas Steele of London would be glad of ten minutes' conversation with him."

You must know that we had arranged this tale on our way from France. He was to be the Comte de Laon; I was to be Sir Nicolas Steele. I had seen the young count chumming a good deal in Paris with the Austrian Horowitz, and I had put Sir Nicolas Steele up to the idea that he should get a letter of introduction from the Austrian to two or three people in Vienna. Once we were in possession of the document (and Horowitz gave it readily enough, although he knew nothing about Nicolas Steele, except that he was the best whip in the city), it was easy enough to scrape out the name of the party whom it favored, and to put in another name. The name we chose was that of Comte de Laon. I will tell you why presently.

So soon as we were in the private office, and face to face with Lobmeyr, I began to reckon up my man. That he was no fool was to be seen with half an eye. His head was long and well-balanced; his eyes were small and keen; he had whiskers which were just turning gray, and those big hands which stamp a man of commanding character. And he didn't bow or scrape like the other chap in the shop, but put on his glasses and read our letter through from end to end before he said a word. I watched him like a cat watches a mouse, and when he stuck for a minute in one place, my heart was in my mouth. But presently he handed the letter back to Sir Nicolas, and the smile on his face told me that all was well.

"Of course," said he, and I'm sure his French wasn't any better than mine, "Count Horowitz is known to me, and any friend of his is welcome. In what way can I be of service to the Comte de Laon?"

"You can sell me a diamond," cried Sir Nicolas, leaning back in his chair like a man who is doing another a favor.

"That is very easily done," said Lobmeyr. "I wish all those who brought letters of introduction to me came upon the same errand. Are you seeking a single stone or a set?"

"I am seeking a single stone, Brazilian if possible, quite white, circular in shape, and weighing not less than fifty carats."

The effect of this speech upon the man was as funny as any thing I ever saw. No sooner were the words out of my master's mouth than Lobmeyr wheeled round his chair and let his spectacles drop upon his knees.

"Fifty carats!" exclaimed he. "Oh, my dear sir, you might go half round Europe and not get such a stone as you seek!"

"Exactly, that is what I said to myself when I was asked by the person whose agent I am to find him such a diamond. 'There are only two houses likely to have so fine a thing,' said I; 'one is Streeter's of London, the other is Lobmeyr's of Vienna.' It is not possible for me to be in London this winter; therefore I go to Lobmeyr."

The man smiled again. He had begun to take the bait like a pike takes a roach.

"Well," said he, "I must justify your confidence in me. I have no diamond in the house which cor- responds exactly to your description, but I have a stone weighing forty-six carats, of which there is no equal in Europe. We call it the Golden Fleece. If you will wait a moment I will show it to you."

Saying this, he swung himself round in his chair again, and opened the great safe which stood behind him. When ten seconds had passed Sir Nicolas had the diamond in his hand, and the whole room seemed full of the sparkle of its lights. So bright, for a fact, was the stone, so magnificent, and of such a size, that even I lost my head at the sight of it, and stood gaping like a child at a wonder. It was just as if the man had taken a fortune from his safe and put it into our hands.

Sir Nicolas was the first to remember himself, and when he did so, he began to speak in such rapid French that I could not follow him. After a bit, however, he checked himself, and then I heard him say:

"In all things except size, it is the diamond I am seeking. Whether size would be a vital objection, the person who commissions me alone could say. He is to meet me to-morrow night at eight o'clock at the Hôtel Métropole. If you will bring the stone there, you shall have a 'yes' or 'no' in ten minutes."

"Are you staying in the hotel?"

"No, I have an apartment for the winter in the Singer Strasse, No. 16, so that we are almost neighbors. But my friend will be at the Métropole to-morrow night, and with your permission we will then take his opinion of the Golden Fleece. The price you said — —"

"Is one hundred thousand florins."

"Ten thousand pounds," said Sir Nicolas, turning to me, and handing me the stone; "do you find it dear?"

I looked at it for some moments through a glass I had brought with me for the purpose. Then I said, in English:

"It is a thousand pounds more than it is worth."

Lobmeyr, it proved, —and this was very lucky for us, —did not understand a word of our own language.

"This gentleman here," cried Sir Nicolas, pointing to me, "who is one of the finest judges in the world of Brazilian stones, is of the opinion that you are asking ten thousand florins too much."

"In that case, M. le Comte, it would be for you to make me an offer of ten thousand florins less. Like all business men, I am open to offers, though I do not say that I will accept them. The diamond I am showing you is the first of its kind in Europe. For exquisite color and shape, for quality generally, I could hardly match it if you gave me a month for the task. It will remain for me to say yes or no when you are prepared to bid for it."

He said it all very sweetly, and when he had done, and the diamond was locked up in the safe again, we arranged for him to bring it to the Hôtel Métropole on the following evening at eight o'clock, and there to ask for the Comte de Laon. Then we got out of his shop, and only when we were under the shadow of the church of St. Stephen did either of us breathe freely again.

"Well," said Sir Nicolas, speaking first, "if Count Laon ever gets to hear that I took his name in Vienna, he'll be admitting that I did him credit. Bedad! I'm just proud of myself."

"You've the right to be that, sir," said I; "and as for Count Laon hearing any thing about it, why should be? He was at his place in Normandy a week ago. I don't suppose there's any thing in the air just now to bring him to Vienna."

"Gospel truth you speak there, and 'tis only for twenty-four hours that we shall be wanting it. Midnight to-morrow should see us out of Vienna."

"With ten thousand pounds in our pockets, and no harm done to any one, sir."

"The devil a bit! Oh, it was a lucky day when you told me to write the history of a diamond-that is, if Benjamin King doesn't draw back. You never know quite whether you've got a Yankee by the tail, or whether he's got you by the teeth. But I've no doubts myself but what he'll buy."

"Nor me, either, sir. They say he never refused to buy a diamond with a history yet."

"And sure, was there ever a better history written than the one we put in the *Figaro* —about a stone that didn't exist, too? Man, it was a colossal notion of yours. If ye don't mind, we'll be off to drink a glass of wine to the health of it."

I had no objection to this, you may imagine; nor could I gainsay him when he declared that the whole thing was my idea. Mine the plan was, mine all through, and never a prettier one born, I'll swear. For, you see, what had brought us from Paris to Vienna was this-we had come to sell to Benjamin King, the American bacon merchant, *a diamond which did not exist.* How the thing came about is told in a few words. I happened to read one day in *Galignan's Messenger* that King had a weakness for collecting historical jewelry. They said he would buy any diamond with a history; and no sooner had I seen the paragraph than I got the notion.

"By the Lord Harry," said I to myself, "you've only got to make up a sham story to palm off on this joker any rubbishy stone at twice its price. Your yarn must be well done, of course, and must have the look of truth about it. But given a steady head and plenty of cheek, there's thousands in the deal."

Well, this was my first inkling of it, but as the day went on, I found the notion working me up into a perfect fever. The more I thought of it, the more money there seemed in it. I convinced myself that you'd only got to plan the thing on a large enough scale to make a fortune. King was a millionnaire; he was in Paris; it was ten to one he would swallow a tempting bait. "If," said I, "we can buy a stone for one thousand and sell it to him for two, there's a thousand pounds. Or, again, if we can buy a stone for ten thousand and sell it to him for twenty because of the sham history we're going to make up about it-where are. we then? Why, ten thousand to the good, and nobody but a swindling old bacon merchant a penny the worse." The idea was colossal, as Sir Nicolas said. It remained only for cool heads and steady nerves to go through with it.

Three days after this notion came to me, there appeared in the Paris *Figaro* a little bit of news which I never should have heard in the ordinary way, but which I read greedily enough under the circumstances. I say that I read it; I should say, perhaps, that I made it out word by word, and chuckled over it like a boy reading his first love-letter. The fact was that Sir Nicolas himself had written it, first in English, then in French; and had sent it along to the paper by one of the writing chaps he used to meet in the Hotel de Lille. It was a short paragraph, but more than enough for our purposes; and as it is necessary to my story, I print the English of it here;

"A MISSING MAZARIN

> "Sir Nicolas Steele, whose devotion to every form of *le sport* has won him the affections of many Parisians, is likely, they say, shortly to offer for sale here a famous white diamond, the history of which is scarcely less eventful than that of the old 'Sancy' stone itself. This is one of the diamonds which Diana of Poictiers wore-one of those stones which Mazarin took, with the 'Mirror of Portugal,' from the Duke of Epernon, to whom they had been sold by Henrietta of France. It will be remembered that the old 'Sancy' stone was stolen in the year 1791. Sir Nicolas Steele has documentary evidence, dating back to the earliest years of the century, that the diamond he now possesses was one of those taken by the mob who sacked the Treasury in the first days of the Revolution. Apart from its most interesting historical associations, the gem is a very fine one, weighing nearly fifty carats, and possessing a lustre only to be found in the choicest treasures of the Brazilian mines."

This is what Sir Nicolas wrote after he had given twenty-four hours' thought to the matter; and I will say that there never was a man who entered into a thing more willingly, or with more spirit.

"Hildebrand," said he, "'tis the idea of a life-time, no less. There's only one corner which frightens me. Where will you be getting your diamond if King takes the bait?"

"You leave that to me, sir," said I. "It's queer if you can't buy a fifty-carat stone somewhere in Paris. And you won't buy it in your own name either. If King came to hear, not only that you were selling diamonds, but buying them, we should have to put up the shutters."

"Ye see far," cried he; "there's few men would have planned it. Yet even now 'tis not all straight to me. You must remember that we've no credit in the place, and who'll be lending us fifty-carat diamonds on our bare word? That's what you're wanting."

"I'm not wanting any thing of the kind, sir," said I. "If this Yankee tumbles into the trap-and the documents we're preparing would deceive the devil himself-he'll either buy or not buy. If he buys, he'll write you a check there and then. You'll have the money in twenty-four hours, and your jeweller will have this. It's strange if he won't wait that long when he hears the tale you can tell, ay, better than any man in Paris."

He began to be convinced at this, and for six days and nights we worked like niggers, getting old musty parchments from Castle Rath, my master's place in Ireland, and writing into them a sham account of the supposed Mazarin diamond. By the time we'd done, we had a pile which would have satisfied all the judges in France; and then only did we communicate with Benjamin King, who was staying at the Hotel Windsor. He replied, by a messenger, saying that he was sorry to miss the opportunity of seeing so famous a diamond, but business compelled him to leave Paris for Vienna that very evening, and he might not be in the city again for three months.

"Was there ever such luck on God's earth?" cried Sir Nicolas, when he heard this tale. "That we should lose him by twenty-four hours! It's enough to make a man shoot himself."

"No such thing, sir," said I. "What is to be done in Paris is to be done in Vienna. For the matter of that, you'll buy the diamond easier there than here, and there won't be so much risk in taking another name. What's to stop you telling King that you also must be in Vienna, say, in a fortnight's time, and will call upon him there? The job's worth the money, any way."

Well, he thought it over, and fourteen days after this talk we found ourselves in the Austrian capital, and at Lobmeyr's shop, as I have told you. Why Sir Nicolas took the name of the Comte de Laon, you know now. To put it short, we meant to *buy* the diamond in that name, and to *sell* it in our own. The count was the intimate friend of Horowitz, a well-known man in Vienna, though then at Rome. We had got letters of introduction from Horowitz, who spent part of his summer holidays in Paris, and we had altered them so that they no longer recommended Nicolas Steele but the Comte de Laon. And armed with these, we began our dealings with Lobmeyr, as you have seen; and it remained only to sell the Golden Fleece to Benjamin King as the identical diamond which Mazarin bought from the Duke of Epernon..

You may ask, and naturally, what were the risks we ran in this, the greatest job of all our lives. I can tell you almost in a word. The risks were two-viz. (1) That Lobmeyr might find out that we were buying a diamond in Vienna under a sham name, and refuse to let the stone go out of his possession; (2) that King might learn the same thing, and decline to believe in our documents. In either case, a visit from the police would be likely to follow the discovery. It is to be understood, therefore, that we preferred private apartments in the Singer Strasse to the publicity of an hotel, and that we had no intention of remaining more than forty-eight hours in Vienna if luck would play the game for us in that time.

It was to our private apartments that we turned when we left the shop in the Graben, and began to see how we stood. So far, fortune was with us. We had found the diamond, we had caught our man. If all went well we might settle with King on the following evening, and be off to Paris again by the midnight train. And if it turned out like that, I knew that we should carry away five thousand apiece as the profit of the venture.

You may imagine that the next twenty-four hours were anxious ones. I went up to the Métropole in the morning and engaged a room in the name of Sir Nicolas Steele, saying that he would dine at the hotel with his friend, the Comte de Laon. That carried out our idea of having two names in Vienna. If any one said to Sir Nicolas, "You are not the Comte de Laon," he had only to point to me; if any one said to me, "You are not Sir Nicolas Steele," I had only to point to my master. For the matter of that, a big hotel is far too busy looking after its guests to be bothering about the identity of people; and no one asked me a single question when I booked the room and ordered the dinner, to which we had already invited Benjamin King, the bacon merchant.

Punctually at seven o'clock that night the three of us sat down to table-Sir Nicolas, King, and myself. My master was clever enough to monopolize most of the conversation, giving it out that I spoke French only; and lucky for me, King's daughter, a pretty little thing I'd seen in Paris, had gone off to the theatre with some friends. I could hold my tongue in her absence, and leave Sir Nicolas to do the blarney, which he did in his own pretty way. King was a big, coarse-made man with a rasping Chicago accent on him; and I think that he was not a little pleased at sitting down with a real Irish baronet and a supposed French count-for, in all our dealings with him, I took the name Comte de Laon, while at the jeweller's I was always Sir Nicolas Steele. Any way, he was civil enough, and when the cigars were lit, he began to talk about the diamond.

"Wal," cried he, "and where's your bull's eye, Sir Nicolas. Out with it! Eh, count,"—and here he turned to me,—"you've heard of the marble he carries in his pocket? Belonged to one of the French queens, he says-Dianner or somebody."

"Indeed, and there's no doubt of it," says my master. "Diana of Poictiers wore it upon her own pretty neck, and so did our own Henrietta. There's no more question that it's a Mazarin than that I am Nicolas Steele of Castle Rath. Ye'll have read the papers, Mr. King?"

"That's so; me and my daughter read 'em yesterday. We haven't got the dust off our hands yet."

"Then you know all I can tell you?"

"I guess we do, and I'm waiting to see your bit of glass. What was the figure you named?"

"One hundred thousand dollars," said my master, without turning a hair. "I'd sooner throw it into the Danube than sell it for less."

"It's a long price," said King, looking serious. "A man must cut a hole in pigs to buy his diamonds at that figure."

"He can buy them for half the sum, if he cares nothing for their history," cried Sir Nicolas quickly. "This stone has no second, but the great Sancy diamond, in all Europe. It has helped to make history; in one way it is priceless."

"Then show it and have done with it," says King, in a mighty proud way.

"There is nothing easier," says my master, "though it is too valuable to carry like a watch in the pocket. My friend Comte de Laon, here, has it at his bankers'. His man is coming up to the hotel at eight o'clock. It should be that and more, now."

With this he turned and said something in rapid French. While I did not understand him, I bowed and smiled as I had been doing all dinner-time; and at that very moment a waiter announced that a gentleman wished to see the Comte de Laon.

We rose together, Sir Nicolas and I; and one quick glance passed between us. Then he turned to King—

"If ye'll sit here for the half of a minute," says he, "you shall hold the stone in your fingers."

"There's no hurry," says King, leaning back in his chair, "though I'd be glad of a green cigar, I guess."

"The waiter shall bring you one," says Sir Nicolas at the door; and with that he pulled me into the passage.

"Remember," cried he in a whisper, directly the door had shut upon us, "we change names again."

"Should I be likely to forget?" says I—and that was all, for the next minute we were down stairs, and the diamond was in Sir Nicolas's hand.

They had shown Lobmeyr into a little room at the side of the dining-hall. I can see him now, wrapped from head to foot in a heavy sable coat, his little eyes dancing like stars as they tried to read us up. He had brought the Golden Fleece in a beautiful shagreen case, and there never was a prettier thing to see than that diamond, I'll stake my life. But events were moving too fast for me to pay any attention to it then, and I was all ears for the talk between the two. One false step, one silly word-and the trick would be blown to the winds. It remained to control our tongues as if curbs of iron held them. Nor, to give Sir Nicolas his due, did he waste any words.

"Before we come to the important question of price, Herr Lobmeyr," said he, after the usual compliments had passed between them, "I'd be glad if I may take the opinion of the friend for whom I am acting in this case. He's at table upstairs, and his judgment and that of other friends with me will help to decide. You will permit me, I am sure, to show the jewel?"

He said this and I felt my heart begin to thump like any thing. If Lobmeyr refused to let the stone go out of his possession, we were done. And he did not give in any too readily. I saw his eyes searching the pair of us through and through. Only after a long pause did he bow an unwilling assent, and Sir Nicolas went off upon the errand which meant all to us.

What passed in the minutes during which he was gone I can't quite tell you. I, for my part, was so excited that I could hardly sit on my chair. As for Lobmeyr, I guessed by his looks that he didn't half like the job. And this was running in my head all the time, that he might refuse to leave the stone behind him until he had the cash in his hand. Possibly Benjamin King might buy the diamond and promise to pay for it next day. If we had to make a fuss, if once King met Lobmeyr and the two understood each other, the bubble would be pricked for good and all; and the sooner we cleared out of Vienna the better. And this thought made me hot and cold in turns. "We must find some way," said I, "to shut his mouth-must give him some security." Yet, what security had we? Nothing but a check-book and our cheek.

All this was in my mind, and I was turning it over and over, pretending at the same time to listen to Lobmeyr's talk, when Sir Nicolas came back again. He had left the diamond behind him, but his looks told me in a minute what had happened. "We have lost the throw," said I to myself; and at this my heart seemed to sink into my boots. As for Lobmeyr, when he saw that his diamond was not in my master's hand, he rose up quick from his chair just as if we had tried to rob him.

"Well," said he, and there was a power of meaning in his tone—"well, M. le Comte, and what do your friends say?"

"That we must have a week to answer you definitely, but that, if we accept the stone, the price you ask will be paid."

The man heard him out, his features gradually relaxing in a smile.

"Nothing could be fairer," said he; "you have only to return me the diamond."

"Ah!" exclaimed. Sir Nicolas carelessly, "I should have explained to you that we are not alone in so large a venture as this. We have others to consult, and we propose that you leave the stone with us until we have their answer."

At this request, the whole look on Lobmeyr's face changed instantly. His eyes seemed to dart fire.

"M. le Comte," said he, "I do not leave this hotel without my diamond or the money for it."

He spoke the words slowly and firmly-but, to me hearing them, they came like a thunderclap. It was just as if he had snatched five thousand pounds from my hands and pitched them out of the window. What to do, what to say, I could not think. I simply stood and stared, imitating my master, whose tongue seemed stuck to his mouth. Meanwhile, Lobmeyr was beginning to work himself up-he raised his voice until you might have heard him on the "third" of the hotel.

"I say that I will not leave the stone," he repeated. "Return it to me or pay me! I will wait here until I receive the money: I will not be put off— —"

He went on like this, just as foreigners will, and really, at one time, I thought he would send for the police on the spot. What with his talk and the talk of Sir Nicolas, who argued and pleaded until he was black in the face, we might have been in a brawl at a fair. But the hullaballoo saved us, for they were in the very middle of it when the idea came to me—

"Offer him a check on the Bank of England," whispered I to Sir Nicolas in a pause; "he'll take that quick enough—a check to be cashed this day week, if we buy."

I said the words, and acting upon them, I pulled out my check-book—for we always had a bit of an account at the Bank-and wrote a check for ten thousand pounds, signing it "Nicolas Babbington Steele," my master's full name. Then I passed it over, without comment, to Lobmeyr.

But I knew that he would take it, for an Englishman's check is still as good as gold in Vienna; and five minutes after the idea came to me, he was out of the hotel, and my master was capering about the room like a village lad with a sugar-stick.

CHAPTER XIV
LOBMEYR APOLOGIZES

The next stage in the story of the great white diamond carries me to the seventh day after the dinner at the Métropole. The situation brought about by the events of that night was a very simple one. King had gone off to Buda-Pesth with the diamond, promising to let us have his answer within the week; Lobmeyr had gone off with a worthless check on the Bank of England, which he was not to cash until seven days had passed. During the between-time we were safe enough, and could go about Vienna as we pleased. But on the seventh morning the danger-bell rang, suddenly and in a way we had never looked for. To put it short, King wrote saying that his return to the Métropole was delayed for five days, but that he would give us a definite answer about the Mazarin directly he was back.

"Hildebrand," said Sir Nicolas, when he read this note, "the game is just up, don't you think? Lobmeyr will never wait another week. And he'll be learning that the check's froth before then. It couldn't have happened worse."

Truth to tell, I was inclined to side with him. I had no fancy to see the shape of an Austrian prison; and yet to clear out of Vienna and leave ten thousand pounds behind us seemed a cruel thing indeed.

"Look here, sir," said I, "the first thing to do is to lie low, and to keep out of our rooms in the Singer Strasse. If the police do get enquiring about us, we may as well have the start of them. I'll take your traps up to that little French hotel by the arsenal during the morning; and after breakfast I'll call on Lobmeyr and see if he won't wait five days. It's strange if he's in all that hurry."

Well, he agreed to this, though he was very gloomy about it; and when I had engaged a room for him at the Hotel Henri IV., booking him as Mr. Winstanley of London, I went down to the Graben, meaning to call upon Lobmeyr. I can remember the events of that morning as if the whole thing happened yesterday-the biting cold, the snow shining crisp in the sun, the hurry-scurry of all who shopped. Nor shall I ever forget the creeping feeling which came over me, when, and just as I was ten yards from Lobmeyr's house, I saw two policemen get out of a cab and go straight in at the door.

Now, if you're engaged on a bit of shaky business,—if for days past you have been saying to yourself, "This will bring me into a law-court or a cell,"—the last thing you care to see is a policeman. I can tell you that for five minutes after I watched those two men get out of the cab and go into Lobmeyr's place, I stood stock still, as if they had glued me to the pavement.

"Good God!" said I to myself, "here's the end of your ten thousand, Bigg, any way. And if you're not precious smart, here's the end of your public engagements for months to come. What's brought those men there, you can't say. Perhaps he's heard that the real Comte de Laon is in Paris; perhaps he's tried to cash the check and got it back again. That don't concern you-what you've got to do is to show your heels and quick about it."

True enough, my first impulse was to run for it, and not stop until Sir Nicolas and I were inside a train for the frontier. A second thought held me back. How was I to be sure, just because I had seen two policemen enter Lobmeyr's shop, that those two policemen were concerned in my fortunes? And it might be, I said, that we could cheat them, even if they were. Once King came back to Vienna, the game was ours. And if we could keep out of the clutches of enquiring busybodies for five days, we might, at the end of that time, tell them to go to the devil or stay at home, just as they pleased.

All this passed through my mind like a flash of lightning while I stood gaping with astonishment at the sight of the policemen. And no sooner had I weighed the matter up than I saw the light through it. Next door to Lobmeyr's there was a meerschaum-pipe shop. A big wooden partition divided the two houses, and to step behind this was the work of a second. But scarce was I in the cover when the two sergeants of police were back again in the cab, and the direction they had given to the coachman was ringing in my ears:

"Singer Strasse Sechzehn."

The gift to gabble in German is not among my acquirements, as you may learn from the story; but German or no German, I don't want any one to tell me what "Singer Strasse Sechzehn" meant.

"They're going straight to our shop to search it," said I to myself; "and that's just the worst thing that could happen to us. They'll find we're missing, and then the fun will begin. Oh, Nicky, Nicky! the devil himself took the tickets when we set out on this job."

You see my mind turned to Nicky at once, for though I had left him snug at the hotel by the Arsenal, I could not say but that he had gone up to his old rooms for the letters, and in that case, the Lord only knew what would follow. I saw that the police might have him even while I was running like a madman to the Hôtel Henri IV. Spurred on by the fear, I flew over the ground like one bewitched. When at last I reached the hotel, he met me on the steps of it, and I nearly knocked him down in my excitement.

"Thank God for this, sir!" said I; and then I told him.

"Ye don't mean to say that," cried he, turning very white.

"Indeed and I do; I saw the cab start with the pair of them inside. There's nothing to be done now but to lie as low as moles. The odds are that they'll search the railway stations and the big hotels; but they'll hardly come to a shop like this."

"That's true," said he; "and yet to think that we wanted only five days of winning! Oh, if King would only come back!"

It was all very well for him to say, "Oh, if King would only come back!" and, for the matter of that, I could almost have prayed for the same thing. King alone could save us. If he turned up, we could pay Lobmeyr or return him his diamond. But King was in Buda-Pesth, and we might as well have prayed for the moon. Meanwhile the police were in the Singer Strasse!

This was how the thing stood-then and for the next three days. The life we lived is not to be told here. Sufficient to say that the pair of us started at every shadow we saw; turned pale every time a waiter entered the room. It's well enough to read in books about haunted men; but I've no fancy myself to play the *rôle*, nor ever had. What I went through at that little Hotel Henri IV. I would not go through again for a thousand pounds, and that's saying something. So badly did the thing wear me, so strangely did it act on my nerves, lying boxed up there like a rat and not knowing from minute to minute whether I was free or a prisoner, that on the third afternoon, at dark, I made up my mind to do something; and I left the hotel while my master was asleep on his bed, worn out with the anxiety and the watching.

You ask me what I was going to do —I'll tell you in a word. I meant to go to the Hotel Métropole and ask for King's address. I thought I would wire to him, or find out, at any rate, exactly when he was returning. As the thing went, however, I did neither, for whom should I see, directly I entered the great hall of the hotel, but King's daughter-the pretty little American girl I had remarked in Paris. There she was, sitting alone at a tea table, a perfect little picture. And two minutes after I saw her she was listening to my story.

"You'll excuse me, miss," said I, "but is Mr. King likely to be in Vienna again soon?"

"Indeed he is not," said she, with a pretty, rippling laugh. "I am afraid he won't be here again at all; he is going straight from Mostar, where he is now, to Trieste. I join him at Venice." If she had struck me, she couldn't have made me reel like her words did.

"Going to Trieste!" exclaimed I, doing my best to hide what I felt; "but he's taking Sir Nicolas Steele's great diamond with him, then?"

She laughed again, appearing to enjoy ray confusion.

"Certainly he is," she said; "but he is leaving the money for it behind him. I have just sent round a draft on the Bank of Vienna."

"You have sent a draft?" I almost shouted, forgetting every thing in the excitement of it.

"Yes," she replied, looking at me very curiously, "to Singer Strasse, No. 16. I sent it ten minutes ago."

"You did!" said I. "Then there's the end of it." It was cruel, look at it as you like. There was the money, which would have done all for us, sent to a house which we dare not go near. I did not doubt that the police had got hold of it already; I was sure that, if we showed our faces to claim it, they would arrest us until the whole thing was explained. The mischief was that we *dare not explain* the whole thing. That would have been to have given ourselves away to King, who might have prosecuted us for obtaining money by false pretences. If ever two men had run into a blind alley, those two men were Hildebrand Bigg and Nicolas Steele.

Something of this must have showed itself in my face to Miss King, for she asked me suddenly if I were ill; and when I assured her that I was not, and managed to stammer out an excuse, I am sure that she thought she was dealing with a madman. Yet for what she thought, or what she did not think, I did not care a brass farthing; and the next thing I remember is that I was tearing up the street leading to the market-place, and that I never stopped until I was opposite our old quarters, and stood gaping up at the window of my master's sitting-room in the Singer Strasse. I had run along with the wild idea that I might overtake the messenger who had the money; but he was coming down the stairs when I reached the house, and a single glance at the lighted windows told me that the deal was lost. I could see a police officer standing by the fireplace. He seemed to be alone in the room, and he had the letter, which had just come, in his hand. I could see him fingering the very draft which would have been liberty and fortune to us. And at that I left prudence behind me and shut my teeth on the resolution.

"I will have that money, if I strangle him for it," said I, and no sooner said than I was on the stairs leading to the flat, and the revolver, which I always carry, whatever be my country, was full cock in my hands. There is no need to think now of all the risks I ran. However many they might have been, I should have faced them, wound up as I was then with greed of the money and despair of the situation. Yet it came to me, even as I mounted the stairs like a cat, that if there were two men in the room, nothing could save me. I carried my liberty, perhaps my life, with me, yet I would have staked them twice over sooner than turn my back on such a prize.

At the top of the stairs I paused a moment, and put my ear to the keyhole of our room. Though I listened for five minutes I did not hear the sound of any voice; and making sure from this that the police officer was alone in the place, I knocked gently with the butt-end of the revolver upon the door. A loud "Herein!" answered me; but taking no notice of this, I knocked again, and at the second knock the door was thrown wide open, and the man was before me. Quick as he was-and he put out his arm to grasp my collar directly he saw me —I gripped him by the throat in such a lightning grip that his eyes seemed to start straight out of his head, and the flesh of his face went all blue and discolored. Never was a man more taken by surprise than he was. He had looked to be the attacking party; I had forestalled him; and now as he reeled back over my knee, and the gurgling in his throat was an awful thing to hear, I forced him into the bedroom close by, and held him on the bed.

"Now," said I, not caring a rap whether he understood English or the other thing—"now, move a hand and I'll shoot you like a dog. What I've come here for is my money. Let me take that, and I'll give you a hundred pounds. But open your lips, and I'll close them with a bullet."

I said this still clutching his throat, and with my knee hard down upon his chest. He was pretty nearly insensible by that time, and when I made sure that he had not strength enough left to give me trouble, I snatched a sheet from the bed and bound it round his face and arms, tying knots which would have held a bullock. A couple of straps, torn off one of my master's trunks, did for his feet; and a length of rope from my box bound him up to the bed. When I had finished with him, I don't believe that he could move his neck an inch either way; and only then did I look for the money. It was lying, fair for all the world to see, on the table by the window. The draft had been in his hand when I knocked at the door; he had simply laid it down when he came to answer me.

Five minutes before closing time that night, we drew our money from the Bank of Vienna. A quarter of an hour later we were in Lobmeyr's shop. I don't think I ever heard a man apologize so much or look so astonished.

"This will teach you," said Sir Nicolas, "to be less hasty in your conclusions, sir. You have done us a very great injury, which I hope you will at once repair."

"Most certainly, I will," exclaimed Lobmeyr, as he turned his notes over and over, and examined them for the tenth time. "I will send to the police at once. But what was I to think? I telegraphed to Rome for the references of the Comte de Laon, and they said that he was not here at all, but in Normandy."

"And can't you understand," cried Sir Nicolas, "that a man may very well give it out that he's in Normandy and yet be in Vienna? Oh, you're a person of small discernment, Herr Lobmeyer! I shall have to call upon the police myself. And that reminds me, we left one of your agents in a bad way up at the Singer Strasse. You can just send up a man to release him, and give him a thousand florins for the inconvenience. Indeed, we had to tie him up to the bed before he would let us have our own money."

"I will do it with pleasure," said Lobmeyr, "and add a hundred florins of my own. I cannot express my sorrow at the whole episode. At any rate, you will have one of the finest diamonds in Europe to be a constant pledge of my regrets."

With this adieu we left him, and drove straight to the station.

"Bedad!" said Sir Nicolas, as we took our tickets, "to think that men could go through what we've gone through these past ten days and yet be gay about it! Hildebrand, ye've made a fortune for me, and I'll not forget it to my dying day."

I couldn't deny this, except that part about the fortune. What we really cleared was three thousand five hundred apiece. Benjamin King, like a true Yankee, knocked three thousand off our original figure, and we didn't make a fuss about the balance, you may be sure.

CHAPTER XV
QUEEN AND KNAVE

There is no date in my diary which tells me exactly when we arrived in Brittany; but I shall not be far wrong if I set it down as the month of March, and, to be particular, rather late than early, in a week when there was spring in the air, and the smell of the country was like new wine to a man. I can remember well that there were many to chaff us for leaving Paris at such a season; and, so far as that goes, it was a queer sort of journey to make just when the town was full of life, and most folks were coming in from the provinces. But Sir Nicolas was hit again, and like many a one before his day, and many a one to come after, time and season were nothing when laid against a woman's pretty face. He would have gone to the other end of the world for Mme. Pauline-aye, I believe he would go now, if it were in his power.

I have seen women enough in my time,—and a man's no worse judge of a pretty girl because fortune compels him to look at her through an attic window,—but this I will say, that a finer creature than the mistress of the Château de l'Épée never drew breath. We had met her first in the Vienna express on our return from that business with Benjamin King,—I laugh now when I think of it,—and she and Sir Nicolas struck up a friendship at once. This was not surprising, for he had the ways which go down with women to a degree I've never seen before or since; and she-well, she was a creature who could walk straight to a man's heart, so to speak. All said and done, it isn't the schoolgirl with the pink-and-white skin, and the simper you find in story-books, that a man of the world cares twopence about, Youth? Yes, he won't turn his head away from that; nor prettiness either, so far as it goes. But it's soul and devil, light and shade, that hold him-and there never was a woman who had them like madame.

I said, when first I saw her, that she was a stranger to the thirties, and this was no wonder, for she had the face of a child. It was not until we had spent some few days in her company that I changed my opinion, and put her down as thirty-one or thirty-two. It's always difficult to read the age of a brunette; and her hair was as dark as night. Not that years made any difference to her; for she was just one of those rare creatures whose acquaintance age seems to shun. There is no greater compliment to a woman than this-that men are glad to hear she is no child. In her case, she was both child and woman, slight and graceful as a young girl should be, gay in talk as one who has not taken a downward rung on the ladder of life. And I never met a man yet who wasn't her servant ten minutes after he knew her.

It is to be imagined how my master carried himself in an affair of this sort. He had seen madame first on the platform at Munich; he was raving about her before we got to Strasbourg; when at last the train drew up at the Gare de l'Est, he spoke to her as though he had known her all his life. I heard him promise to call upon her immediately at her apartment in the Rue de Lisbonne. He couldn't talk of any thing else for hours after.

"Indeed, and 'tis lucky entirely I am to have travelled in that same train," said he to me, directly we were alone together in the cab. "Was there ever the like to her born? She's Mme. Pauline Sainte-Claire, the sister to the artist of that name, I'd have you know. Her husband died at Brest three years ago — —"

"Oh," said I, for I saw how the land lay, "they always die like that."

But at this he flared up in a minute.

"If it's any insult you mean to her," cried he, "you'll go out of the cab this minute. Was there any need to remind ye that ye're a servant?"

"None at all," said I, though I could have have hit him for the word. "A servant I am; maybe an indispensable one"—and with that I looked him full in the face, and he turned as white as a sheet.

"'Tis late in the day to quarrel, isn't it?" he asked.

"You're the best judge of that, sir," said I.

After this we rode on to the hotel without a word; but he went the same afternoon to leave his card in the Rue de Lisbonne, and the next night he dined there. I knew at once that this was no ordinary affair, for he had brought plenty of money in his pockets from Vienna; and when he began to go to madame's house almost as regularly as I went to the Café Rouge, I said to myself that he was tied up for the winter, at any rate. And so it proved. Christmas passed, and still found him dancing attendance. He was harder hit than ever at the end of January. The matter seemed to come to a head in March, when he began, all of a sudden, to order clothes enough to stock a tailor's shop, and to make preparations for leaving Paris.

Now, during all these weeks he had never said a word to me of the woman, or of his own intentions about her. Whether he remembered our bit of a difference at the Gare de l'Est, or whether he had something in his mind which he did hot want me to know, I never found out. And though I did my best to get an inkling of what was going on in the Rue de Lisbonne, I never succeeded. You might as well have tried to pump an East End waterworks as the *concierge* of. that hotel. The only servant Mme. Pauline had was a saucy bit of goods, who could roll out lies like an auctioneer. Watch the place as I did-and my eyes were rarely off it in my leisure hours —I never learned more than common-sense had told me at home. Twice a week he dined with her, or she dined with him. For the rest, they went to the theatre, but always with a third party; they skated together; they were seen in the parks; yet so careful was she of her reputation that a bishop could not have found fault with her. I thought at the start that she might be trying to get his money over the card-table —but here I was right down wrong, and don't believe he staked threepence the whole winter through. It's fair to say that she led him into no other extravagances. He spent less money that quarter than he had done for years-drank less, and was better tempered.

This is how the thing went on until March; and when that month came I had given it up as a mystery. It seemed to me that he was just in love with the creature's pretty face and pretty ways, and that was all you could say about it. I concluded that he would end by marrying her, and that I should find myself compelled either to serve a mistress-which I could never do-or to begin life afresh with what capital I had made in his service. In fact, I was just looking about to see what sort of a future I could make for myself, when he burst upon me with the news that we were going into the country, and that our destination was Brittany.

"It's not the time I'd be choosing to leave Paris," said he, "but we won't be away a month, and there'll be fun when we return. Ye must know that she's a great place in Brittany, at the woods of Folgöet it is, and we're to take the night train to Châteaulin on Monday. Will I be wanting clothes, do you think?"

I told him that he had suits enough to last him ten years, for I was never one that hungered after old coats; but he was not to be put off that way.

"'Tis true enough," said he, "yet I doubt the shape of them entirely. There's great folk to meet-the Duc de Marmontel, he's coming — —"

"Oh," said I, "is that the one they wouldn't have at the Jockey Club last year?"

"The same," said he, "and a rare devil for the play, they tell me. Then there's Prince Paul, the Russian; and Lord Beyton, son of the Earl of Lomond, you'll remember. Bedad! it's pleasant company altogether, though a man would do well not to finger the cards with them."

"You're right there, sir," said I, "though I don't doubt there will be cards in Brittany."

"Not at all," said he; "she'll have nothing to do with them. Her brother, the Comte de Faugère, told me so yesterday. They say that he's going for the Church, though I have my doubts. Ye must remember that she herself is the widow of an artist, and fond of gay folk. I make sure she'll amuse us finely."

There was no good arguing with him, for he was set upon it, and, to cut a long story short, we were in Brittany and at madame's château on the following Tuesday morning. I said at once that a prettier place never was; nor one with such green hills and sweeping forests. Mile after mile we drove from the station through woods which man never seemed to tread. There were mazy paths and leafy groves, turn where you would. The house itself was like an old shire mansion, low and gabled, with a white spire at the north end of it, and lawns smooth as billiard tables before its windows. The company, so far as names went, was beyond talk; and by far the best ornament to be found the whole house through was Mme. Pauline, who looked for all the world like a pretty schoolgirl broken out of bounds to enjoy herself. Think as I would, I could find no fair reason to quarrel with my quarters or the woman who found them for me; nevertheless I had my doubts about the journey from the start-could make nothing of it, in fact, and was the more suspicious on that account.

"What's her game?" I kept asking myself. "What is she doing down here with a company like this, when all the world is going back to Paris? If she was just in love with him, why not finish the business in town? He was willing enough."

This I said, turning the thing over and over in my mind, the very first night we came to the Château de l'Epee, which was her place.

I should tell you that they had lodged me with two or three more gentlemen's gentlemen in a little pavilion standing out in the park, about two hundred yards from the big house itself. I was never one that cared for society in a servants' hall, especially when that society was French down to the finger-tips; and when I had made sure that none of the others knew more than I did, either about Mme. Pauline or her party, I left them alone and went my own ways. So it came about, on the second night after we arrived at the house, that eleven o'clock struck and found me walking in the great park which surrounded the château. It was dark enough then for any thing, the cloud hanging low over the woods, and a warm south wind promising rain. But the blinds were up in most of the lower rooms, and I had not taken ten steps to cross the lawn when I solved my mystery. Mme. Pauline's guests were playing roulette.

"Halloa!" said I, standing stock still, and laughing to think how simple it was, "so this is your game, is it, my lady? You brought him here to dance on the green, eh? And he's fool enough to come up smiling, like a lamb to be sheared. I wonder if you heard that he picked up money at Vienna-it looks like it, any way."

Certainly, it did look like it, for there he was, hanging over the cloth like a boy over a rail; and throwing the money away, I did not doubt, just like a man pitching pebbles into the sea. As for the others, they were as deep in it as they could be; old Marmontel sitting with a pile of gold at his elbow, and young Lord Beyton throwing the notes about as though they were spills. Yet-this was curious-madame herself was not playing. She was sitting at the piano strumming a waltz; and though I watched her for nearly an hour, never once did I see her turn her eyes toward the table. She was acting the simple little girl still-and right well did she play the part.

Now, when you have looked for something really deep and surprising in a puzzle, it does not please you to find that its solution is plain enough for a schoolboy. For the matter of that, once I saw the ball spinning in the Château de l'Épée, the only thing that remained for me to know was the name of madame's partner in the deal. That she had a partner, probably the man who kept bank, was certain. They went shares, I said, in what they could win from the pigeons they had caged. Probably, too, the thing was square enough, or an old bird like Marmontel would not be throwing his money away so cheerfully. Tricks would not pay in that house of rooks. If my master walked out of the château a beggar, he would have his own luck to blame. And that he would walk out a beggar, I felt sure from the start.

I had come to this conclusion, standing in the park of the château, and smoking my pipe under the shadow of a great elm-tree on the lawn before the drawing-room windows. It was not a conclusion to put me in good spirits, or to send me to bed in a cheerful mood-and so far as that goes, I found myself presently thinking very much about it, and strolling through the ground as I did so. For one thing, you see-money to be made or money to be lost, I saw no chance of my coming into the business. If Sir Nicolas was bitten both by the woman and the cloth, Heaven knew how long he would stay at the house. That he had any other danger to fear I did not then believe. The mystery had proved the cheapest affair possible; there could be nothing behind it.

It was curious, upon my life, but these words were hardly off my lips when I saw something in the grounds of the Château de l'Épée which altered in a moment my whole opinion of our situation, and set my brain itching with curiosity. My walk had carried me perhaps a mile from the house. Thinking of nothing but Mme. Pauline's prettiness and of her schemes, I looked up presently to find myself in a clearing of a wood, and almost at the door of a little pavilion built in the heart of the thicket. There were no lights in the windows of this strange little house, nor any thing to tell that any one lived in it — but all in a moment, while I was standing in the shadow of the trees, a man crossed the grass before the door, and let himself into the pavilion with a latchkey. For ten seconds at the most I saw him, and though there was nothing but a fitful play of the moonlight between the rolling clouds, I recognized him at once. He was Mme. Pauline's brother-the man who passed in Paris as the Comte de Faugère.

"Come," said I to myself, stepping back into the thicket, "what are you doing here, young man, and why don't you show yourself in the house? She gave it out that you had gone back to your seminary, or whatever you call it. How does it happen that you can't show your mug in public? It's a queer state of things, any way."

Queer it appeared to be, look at it how you like. Here was a boy, who, according to madame's story, was being trained for a priest, —one whom we all thought to be in Paris, —masquerading at midnight in the woods of the château. More than that, he was not masquerading alone, for I had not watched the pavilion for ten minutes when I saw another lad, slim and rather short, and wearing a soft felt shooting hat, slip out of the shelter of the trees, and knock three times upon the door of the little building. The door was opened at once; but, although there were now two of them in the house, not a light did I see. Back and front, the place was as dark as the grave, and as mysterious. Not a sound of any thing human was to be heard. You might have passed the pavilion a hundred times and never have known that a living thing occupied it. You might have walked for a month in the park and yet have been ignorant that such a nest was a part of it. Whatever were his reasons, the Comte de Faugère had a roosting-ground which many a hunted man might have envied.

CHAPTER XVI
AT THE PAVILION IN THE WOOD

I have written it above that this discovery altered my opinion of the Château de l'Épée and of its mistress just about as suddenly as a man's opinion could be altered. It is one thing to believe that you're asked to a house to play cards; it is another to wake up to the fact that you are the guest of queer folks who can't afford to be seen in the daylight, and whose object in lying low doesn't altogether explain itself. That the Comte de Faugère was lying low, I never had a doubt from the start of it. And yet this continued to be the puzzle-that he was at the château, while they gave it out that he was in Paris.

It was daylight that morning before I went to sleep. There were moments when I said that I would have it out with Sir Nicolas Steele before another day was passed; other moments when I remembered what a poor hand he was at holding his tongue, and resolved that I would get deeper down into it before I shared it with him. "Maybe," said I, "it doesn't concern us any more than the pump in the court yonder; maybe it concerns us very much indeed.

In either case, his is not the head to deal with it, for he's blind set on the woman and won't listen to reason."

This thought prevailed in the end, and I went to shave him in the morning just like a man got up from a long night's sleep. I found him irritable and not over disposed to talk; and I could see that he had been losing pretty heavily the night before. In fact, he was almost dressed before he said any thing at all, and then he spoke short and almost curt.

"Is it good quarters ye have below?" he asked.

"The best," said I; "they've put us out at the little place in the park yonder."

"Ay, 'tis the picture of a house," said he, "and some very pretty company in it."

"That's so, sir," said I; "there must be a wonderful lot of money on this very landing."

"Ye speak truth," cried he; "the duke alone has enough to buy a kingdom."

"So I've been told," said I, trying my best to draw him out; "and a rare one for cards he is, they tell me."

"I'll not deny it," he exclaimed, as he took the towel from my hands; "he plays like a gentleman."

"Like a what, sir?" said I, sudden, for I couldn't keep the thing back.

"Like a gentleman," he answered, very slow and deliberately, "and it's me that should know, for I lost three hundred to him last night."

"I'm sorry to hear that, sir," said I, "and madame not liking the play, either."

"Sure, she doesn't like it at all; but what could she do in her own house when the duke brings out his cloth, and says, 'Just one game for the luck of it?' Faith, he carries a board wherever he goes, and you might as well expect a child not to touch the jam as to keep his fingers off it. And 'tis wonderful luck he has, too. He won on manque fifteen times running last night. I've never seen the like."

"Let's hope his luck will change, sir," said I, as he put on his coat to go down stairs; "we couldn't afford many nights like that."

"Indeed, and we couldn't, and she'll not be allowing it, either. She detests the play entirely-and no wonder, with a brother that's half a Jesuit, and the lesson her husband taught her not yet forgotten. He lost a fortune at the cards in Paris, ye may know. Bedad! they say he would have played with the priest that came to anoint him."

This was all the talk we had that day, for he spent the morning riding in the woods with Mme. Pauline; and when he dressed for dinner at night he was in such a fluster to make himself fine that I could not get a word with him. As the thing stood, he could not tell me any thing which would help me to get to the bottom of the mystery in the park; and that was the matter my mind ran upon. Hour after hour I'd been thinking of it, yet not a foot further had I got; and I was just about burning with curiosity when eleven o'clock at night came, and I set off through the woods to take a second look at the pavilion. This time, however, I went warily, creeping like a shadow through the trees; and once at the little house, I did not content myself with watching it from the thicket opposite, as I had done the night before; but I lay down boldly at that side of it nearest the wood, and so placed myself that I could not only see my man, but hear him. And this I did without danger. The windows of the place looked out back and front; there was a thick bush to hide my body; and a great shadow, for the moon shone bright and clear, lying half over the lawn in the clearing. I was as safe from sight as a bird in the corn; the place could not have served me better if I had planned it myself.

Half an hour, perhaps, I lay thus crouching upon the grass before I heard any sound or saw any more. But, and this just when I was thinking that I had come out on a fool's errand, there was then a low whistling in the trees, and the door of the pavilion opened to let out the Comte de Faugère. At the same moment, the lad who had met him on the previous evening sprang out from the shadows of the copse, and stood a minute with the moonlight shining brightly on his face. I say "his face," but it should be "her face." The pair had not been there ten seconds when I recognized both of them. For the new-comer was no other than Mme. Pauline dressed up in boy's clothes. And the man she came to meet made no bones at all about his welcome; he took her in his arms and kissed her for five minutes together.

You may think that this discovery surprised me. I can never remember any thing in all my life which so completely knocked me over. For minutes together my brain was in a perfect whirl. Who, then, I asked myself, is the Comte de Faugère? why does his sister wear a man's clothes and meet him at twelve o'clock at night in a wood? why does he kiss her like a boy-lover kissing a schoolgirl? A hundred answers flashed upon my mind-one as impossible as the other—a hundred speculations were raised only to be put aside again. Listen as I would, I could get no help from the talk between them. For a long time nothing but stray words came to me; when at last the pair turned toward the house together, the few sentences I put together were so much Greek.

"Jean leaves to-morrow," said she, and I could see that their arms were locked together; "it will be forty-eight hours, I fear."

"What of Marmontel?" said he in answer to this.

"A week should work that," she replied; "but he is an old fool."

They walked a few more steps in silence, and then, just as they were at the door, he said;

"It was understood about the signals and the lantern."

"Of course it was-and the wine," she answered; and with this on her lips, she disappeared into the pavilion with him. I heard him lock the door-and then, precisely as it was on the first night I had seen them, there was a dead silence in the woods, and every living thing seemed to have fled.

"Bigg," said I to myself, crawling at last from my hiding-place, "if ever you ran against a stone wall, this is the day. You can make as much of it as you could of a mummy. The best place for you is bed-and after that Paris."

I made up my mind to this, and, buttoning my coat round me, I ran back sharply to the château. It was all too new, too surprising for me to make head or tail of it, and I do believe that I ran all the way to the great house, with the word "signals" ringing in my ears. When at length I did stop, I was gasping for breath on the lawn before the drawing-room windows; and I saw, as I stood, that Mme. Pauline's guests were still round the roulette board. But she herself was not there,—I knew she could not be,—and as for the others, the only one who interested me was Sir Nicolas himself. It did not take me very long to learn how it had gone with him. One glance at his face told me the story. He had been losing heavily again.

For five minutes, perhaps, I watched the party, and being certain at last that nothing more was to be gained by cooling my heels on the lawn, I went up to my bit of a bedroom and lay down, dressed as I was, to think. I knew well enough that I should have little sleep that night; but it was not until I began to work right through the story that I learned what a task I had set myself. For, you see, I could not get a starting-point. If the woman had asked us down there to skin us, how came it that Marmontel always kept the bank? He was not her confederate, that I was ready to swear. And how did this supposition fit in with the little box in the park and a brother who took the girl in his arms just like a soldier cuddling a housemaid? It didn't fit anyhow, I said. Look at it as you would, there was no light through it. Of one thing only was I sure-Mme. Pauline was no sister to the Comte de Faugère. Yet how did that concern our fortunes?

CHAPTER XVII
THE REHEARSAL

These were the things that were in my mind the whole night through, and what sleep I got did not come to me until the sun was streaming through the windows and the birds in the park were singing fit to split your ears. I had made up my mind then that the business was beyond me, and that I could only watch and wait and make use of what I had seen when the opportunity came. As for telling my master, the idea was farther from my mind than ever. When I went to his room at eight o'clock, I did my best to look like a man who is thinking of nothing but his breakfast, and who will think of nothing after that but his dinner.

"Good-morning, sir," said I. "Are you ready for me now?"

"The devil a bit!" said he, sitting up in bed and looking very pale; "'tis like a boiled owl I feel."

"You made a night of it, then?" said I.

"Indeed and we did, and I lost fifteen hundred."

"You did, sir?"

"'Tis truth I speak. Fifteen hundred last night and three hundred the night before!"

"That's a heavy bill for two days in the country, sir."

"Faith, too heavy for me. And if ye'd bring me a brandy-and-soda, I'd be the better for it. I've to ride with madame this morning."

I brought him the spirit, and when he had drunk it he seemed more himself.

"Hildebrand," said he, getting up suddenly off the bed, "'tis a beautiful air to breathe, but too strong for me. I think we'd do better in Paris."

"I'm sure of it, sir," said I, glad to hear him talk like that.

"But better or worse, I'll be staying a while yet," said he, after a minute; "there's business that keeps me, and, bedad! 'tis pleasant business too."

I knew what he meant, and there was no need to talk to me in this way. The business that kept him at the château was madame's pretty face. He followed it everywhere, riding with her in the morning, taking tea with her in the arbor by the lake in the afternoon, turning over her music at night, looking into her eyes whenever they met as if he could have eaten her. And all the time she was the wife of another man-and more than that, was as deep down in roguery as any scoundrel out of Newgate. I write that she was deep down in roguery, but that is to get ahead in my story. You want to know, naturally, how I found that out, and I will tell you in a few words. It was the second day after I had seen the strange thing in the woods —a day when I was beginning to say that whatever was the mystery of the château de l'Épée, I should never unravel it. I had spent the morning brushing up my master's clothes; but in the afternoon I carried a message down to the village, and as I was returning through the park I chanced to pass at the back of the little arbor by the lake. Sir Nicolas was sitting there with Mme. Pauline, but instead of making love to her as usual, he was watching her spin a little ball in a basin. This seemed to me such a funny thing that I stopped a minute to watch; and observing that no one was about, I crept quite up to the place presently, and got a better view of what she was doing. I found then that what I had taken to be a basin was nothing but a bit of a roulette board, and that madame was showing him how well she could keep bank.

"Look," she said, and her eyes were as bright as diamonds when she spoke, "I will spin any number you like. Choose one yourself, and try me."

He named the number twelve, and she set the ball rolling. When it stopped, I knew by his exclamation that she had succeeded.

"Faith, it's like a miracle!" cried he. "Was it here that you practised it?"

"Indeed no! I learned it when I used to be *tailleur* for my husband. They played almost every day then, and I spun the ball so often that I found out at last how to make it go into any hole I pleased. What a fortune I could win if I were dishonest!"

With this she drew quite close to him, and I saw him wind his arm tight round her. Presently she said, and said it very sweet, too;

"Marmontel has won a great deal off you, hasn't he?"

"The matter of four thousand," replied he, very gloomily.

"You would win it back, and more, if I were to spin the ball to-night, and you were my partner," she went on, still very nicely.

"You're mocking me!" said he in French, but his face flushed with the word; "the thing's not possible."

"Not possible!" said she, looking up at him in her saucy way—"not possible, when two of the croupiers at Monaco made a fortune out of it last year. Oh, Sir Nicolas Steele, how simple you are!"

"But it's a new idea to me," said he, and he was excited too. "Will you show it to me once more?"

"What number will you have?" asked she.

"Twenty-seven for luck!" cried he.

I saw her take the little ball in her hand and spin the basin. When at last it stopped, Sir Nicolas gave a great cry and jumped up off his seat.

"There's a fortune in that," said he.

"Without doubt, for those that know how to use it," was her answer.

"You mean — —" said he.

But what she meant I never heard, for they had both risen from their seats, and I thought it about time to make off. She was locking the little basin in one of the cupboards of the arbor when I left them, and he was bending over her, earnest in talk. I fancied, however, as I went along, that I could have told him as much as she could, and, truth to tell, the few words I had heard had knocked the bottom clean out of all my speculations.

"Bigg," said I to myself, "if ever you're starving, don't go to think that you'll make a fortune out of keyholes. Why, what's it come to? You've been asking all along who's her confederate, and here she's choosing Nicky himself for the part. If it don't beat cock-fighting, I'm a Dutchman."

Take it as I would, I must say that it did alter in a moment all my theories about the château and its pretty mistress. So long as I had looked to find my master a victim of the woman, so long did I suspect every man and every move in and out of the great house. But once it came home to me that she had invited us there to help her, then the whole game was clear to me. The comte, I was sure, dare not show in the house because some of madame's guests knew him to their cost. Nicky was chosen for the part as a man who wouldn't stand at much, and who would cover madame's tricks. As for her being able to throw what number she liked-well, it's all history that a croupier did it at Monte Carlo last winter. "But," said I, "only the very devil of a woman would have gone so deep"—and that was gospel truth.

It was about five o'clock when I got back to my room, and I did not see Sir Nicolas again until the gong went for dressing. He was silent, as usual, but he did not hide it from me that his nerves were all on the twitch; while the slap-dash way he put on his clothes was a tale in itself. When at last he did go down, he shouted to me that he should want me no more that night, and that possibly we should be going back to Paris next morning-at which I laughed to myself, as well I might.

"You'll go back to Paris with full pockets, Nicky," said I to myself; "but you won't be so pleased when you learn more about the chap yonder, and the kissing he does in the wood. Love's a very pleasant business, but it don't do to take partners."

I was still laughing over the notion when I put his clothes away and went down to my own supper. There was plenty of time before me,—for I meant to see the play in the drawing-room that night,—and it was not until ten o'clock was chimed from the spire of the château that I lighted my pipe and went out into the grounds. But I was doomed to a big disappointment. For the first time since I had been at the house, the shutters of the room were closed. Not a ray of light passed them. You couldn't hear a sound, standing on the lawn as I did. All the folks might have packed up their bags and gone back to the city. The place might have been as deserted as the grave.

I was annoyed at this, you may be sure, and having nothing particular to do, I took a stroll through the woods toward the little pavilion where I had seen and heard so many queer things. But here, for the second time that evening, all was changed. The door of the little house was wide open. Inside it was dark as death. More than that, I had not taken twenty steps on my way home through the thicket when I came across something which I had heard of before, but the recollection of which had gone clean out of my head. It was a red lantern swinging at the branch of a tree.

"Halloa!" said I, and I suppose that I spoke aloud, "so here's the lantern you asked after, my friend-and red too. Well, if I know any thing of that color, it means danger."

Now, I'm not a timid man, but when you speak to yourself, believing there's no one within a mile of you, it does give you a start to get an answer. And the words were scarce off my lips when some one in the wood at my right hand called out to me, and in good English too;

"Yes, that means danger, Bigg."

"Who the devil are you?" said I, turning round sudden, but seeing nobody.

"I'm from across the Channel-but not on your job, Bigg, so don't trouble yourself. It's the Comte de Faugère I'd be glad to shake hands with."

Saying this, a little man dressed in a bowler hat and a short black coat sprang out of the thicket and faced me. I guessed how things stood in a minute-detective was written all over his face.

"Well," said I, "so you want the count?"

"I do," said be, "and pretty badly; but it's not this time, I fancy. He's a hundred miles from here by this."

"And his wife — —"

"Be d — —d to her!" said he. "She's the cleverest woman I ever met, and she's done me again, I reckon. You give your guv'ner the tip. If he makes any money up yonder let him tie up his breeches pocket tight. If he don't, she'll steal every penny of it "

"Do you say that?" cried I.

"I do so," said he. "If I was him, and I had any winnings hanging about, I'd bank 'em at Brest, and take thundering good care they didn't go by her messenger. But you don't want to be told twice."

I said that I did not, and after a few words of thanks to him-for he'd put me all in a fever —I ran back to the house, determined that Nicky should know the whole story before another hour had passed. In this attempt luck favored me for the first time. I found my master walking on the lawn with young Lord Beyton. They were smoking together, and seemed to be in earnest talk.

"Well, Hildebrand," said Sir Nicolas, when he saw me, "what keeps you up at this time of night?"

"A letter you gave me to-day, sir," said I. "Could I speak to you about it for a minute?"

He took the hint, and, leaving Beyton, he walked across the lawn with me. Before we took the second turn, I had told him the story.

"Good God!" said he, turning very pale. "Are ye sure of it?"

"As sure as you're talking to me."

"And the man's her husband?"

"Something like that," said I.

"The little witch!" cried he, though it was plain that the news hit him hard.

"But I've the matter of two thousand in notes, and promises for as much more in my pockets now," he went on after the pause. "Ye must know that I had the luck to-night when she came to the table."

"If that's the case, sir," said I, "the sooner the money's in the bank at Brest, the better for us."

"Ye speak truth," exclaimed he; "but who's to take it?"

"I'll start at dawn," said I; "meanwhile there's no need for me to go to sleep. I'm used to a night out of bed now and then."

"And what should I do?"

"Go on as usual, but take the first train to Paris in the morning. I don't fancy the police as footmen myself-nor you neither, I imagine?"

He said that he did not, and when he had given me the money-and the promise of two hundred and fifty if I got through safe with it-he went back to the others as I had suggested. But I returned to my room, and locking myself in, I waited for the dawn like a sick man. Many anxious nights I have passed in my life, but that was the worst of them all. Every whistle of the wind on the staircase, every creak of board or bed set my nerves agog. It seemed to me that I should never get out of the house with the money-perhaps not with my life. A hundred times I must have gone to my window to watch the park; a hundred times I thought I heard footsteps on the staircase, and opened my door to listen. Yet the first gray of daylight found me still where I was. Not a soul appeared to be in the grounds of the château. The old house loomed up out of the cold mists like a great deserted temple. Look where you would, you could see nothing but the trees and the green of the grass. The only sound was the shrill twittering of the birds in the bushes.

Ten minutes after the dawn had come, I left my room and set out upon the journey. I had tied the money round my waist, and had loaded my revolver before I started; but once in the park, these precautions, and my fear all night, looked pretty foolish. It was plain that I was the only man then about Mme. Pauline's place. Even the cattle were still lying upon the wet grass; the horses still sleeping in the meadows. As it was in the gardens, so I found it in the woods. The night keepers had gone to their beds; the dairymen were not yet out of doors. A beautiful stillness was everywhere, a freshness of the morning which was like champagne to a man. I had not walked a mile before my spirits came back to me, and I began to laugh out aloud at the little chap in the bowler hat who had put the thing into ray head the night before.

"Good Lord," said I, "that you should fluster a man so, when I dare say she had no more thought of doing such a thing than of marrying Nicky! But that's always the way with policemen-they aren't content with what their eyes can see, but want to look at it through a microscope. Rob him? Not she, so long as he'll play for her."

I was pretty well through the wood at this time, and when the sun began to shine it found me on the high-road leading to the railway station. I had walked perhaps a mile down this when I saw a man on ahead of me, going my way, but slower than I was; and at the second look I recognized him. He was the little detective I had laughed at.

"Halloa, there!" I shouted, mighty glad to get company in my walk, "what are you doing abroad at this time of the morning?"

He waited for me to come up to him, and then he cried;

"Why, it's Bigg-and in a hurry, too!"

"You've put your thumb on it," said I. "And you didn't catch the count, I make sure, or you wouldn't be here."

"Catch him!" exclaimed he; "no, not quite. You don't take birds like him in the nest. He's too many sentinels."

"Is the charge a heavy one?" I asked as we walked along together.

"Obtaining a diamond in London," said he; "but there's a dozen others. He's a bad one right through, is the Comte de Faugère."

I said that he must be, and then we both quickened up a bit.

"I'll be coming over here after Nicky Steele, by and by, I fancy," he remarked pleasantly, when we had covered a mile or more.

"Ah," said I, "it will want a sharp man for that job!"

"I won't deny it," cried he; "the way that chap keeps outside the law is a crusher. Here's a health to him!"

He had pulled a silver flask out of his pocket as he spoke, and raised it to his lips. Then he passed it over to me.

"Brandy, mate," said he; "you can't do better in the raw of the morning."

I took a good nip, for the day was bitter cold, and gave him back his flask. But I had not walked on ten yards when I found myself reeling like a drunken man-and then I fell heavily, with him bending over me.

One night, some ten days after I fell down insensible on the road to Brest, Sir Nicolas and I were talking in my bedroom in the village of Folgoet of Mme. Pauline and her château. I was still weak and bruised and unable to leave my bed, and he had come up to say good-night to me.

"All!" said he, "we'd be four thousand the richer to-day if you had never discovered that the Comte de Faugère had a liking for the woods."

"Say, rather, sir, if one of his gang had not played it off on me that he was a detective."

"Ye're right there. To give it out that he was an English officer, too! 'Twas a daring business altogether-for the French police were watching the house the very night when the woman stayed for a last deal. The count must have gone the day before. She left in the middle of the night, after I'd won the money for her. 'Tis the Lord only knows how she got away."

"I can tell you, sir, for I saw her in the woods one day disguised as a man. That's how she cheated them."

"I don't doubt it," said he; "they had sentinels everywhere, and used flags by day and lanterns by night for the danger signals. Sure, she was a wonderful woman-to rent a house like that and to play the part."

"Any way," said I, "her man nearly did for me."

"Indeed and he did. There was not much life in you when the priest found you, and carried you to the village."

"And not much money, either."

"They'd not left you sixpence for a cab-fare," cried he.

CHAPTER XVIII
I LEAVE MY MASTER

It was early in the summer of last year when Sir Nicolas Steele and I took different roads in life. They tell me that he has now settled down in a little village near Pau; but from him I hear nothing. It may be that my company would trouble him in these days; it may be that he would be very glad to see me if I knocked on his door. Those are questions I don't care to ask myself. Marriage changes a man, they say. Possibly it has changed him.

It was the summer of the year when I left him; and the early autumn brought me to America. I knew that there was breathing room across the water; and once I had done with Nicky Steele, I did not lose much time in putting the sea between me and those who troubled themselves with my concerns. And that's a step I have never regretted. There's room for every man in the States, so long as he carries a decent head on his shoulders and a bit of brass in his pocket. They don't ask you there if you came by your own honestly. Character is a cheap article, and reputation is put by in museums.

I sailed for America, and it was there that I wrote these papers. They won't hurt Sir Nicolas Steele-and if they do, that's his business. Mine is to make the money while I can; but as for what the law can do to me, I don't care a snap of the fingers. So far as that goes, I doubt if there's much in our past that any judge could spout upon. All said and done, it's easy to be a rogue by Act of Parliament. If Nicky and I got our dues, we should have a statue all to ourselves on St. Stephen's Green, and our portraits would be hung in the Kerry town hall. But this is a short-sighted world, and it knows nothing of its greatest men.

It is a year ago since I left my master, and many things have happened since then-though none of them so odd as the events which led up to that parting. We had returned to Paris quietly enough after our fool's errand to Brittany, and there was no thought in our heads of any thing but a slow season and an unprofitable summer. Such of our friends as had been useful had gone their ways, some to Lon- don, some to America. There was no pigeon to pluck that I knew of; no Yankee who would buy diamonds. Sir Nicolas had little to do but drive and play with the old impecunious lot; and right well lie did it.

"While the money's left, be hanged to the care!" he would say; and for the matter of that, all the lifebelts in France couldn't have saved that same dull care when he set out to drown her. Time and again I told him that if nothing was to be done in Paris, we might find work enough in Madrid or in Berlin. He wouldn't so much as listen to me.

"Is it a bagman I am?" he asked one day when I was harping on the old string again. "Must I be running round the country seeing who'll buy me wares? Indeed, and I'll stop where I am "

"Until the money is spent, sir," I hinted.

"A curse upon the money!" said he. "It's nothing but the money you think of the week through. Am I a pauper, then? And who's to put gold in me purse in Germany? Bedad! I'd as soon spend a week in the Mazas as in that same country. There was no gentleman ever came out of Germany-no, nor honest liquor either. I'd be dead in a week of their beef."

I did not answer him, for he never was a man you could persuade when he was in one of his tempers. He dined that night at the Hôtel Scribe with Jack Ames and his lot; and it was not until one o'clock in the morning that I saw him again. He was pretty well warmed up with the drink then, and directly he set eyes on me, he called out at the top of his lungs;

"Hildebrand, it's yourself I want and no other; fetch me the whiskey, and don't ye sing hymns on the way."

I got him the drink, and when he had pulled out a great handful of cigars and dropped half of them on the pavement, he burst out with his news.

"Man," said he, "it's fine intelligence I have for ye. We're to be in St. Petersburg in three days!"

"Be where, sir?" I gasped, for I made sure that he was joking.

"In St. Petersburg, and nowhere else," replied he, holding the match about a foot away from his cigar—"in St. Petersburg, I'm telling ye. I've a fancy to see the Russians, and there's one of Jack Ames' lot that will take us through. It's an officer of the' Guards he is, and ye'll not forget to pack me yeomanry clothes, though the Queen-God bless her! — has dispensed with my services."

"Then it's certain that you are going, sir?" said I.

"As certain as the moon is round," cried he, "which is a geographical fact, Hildebrand."

What more he would have said I don't know, for he broke off sudden and went to bed,— which was the best place for him,—singing and swaggering like a trooper of the line. I thought at the time that he was telling me some whim of his cups; but when the morning came, he had still head enough to repeat the story and to remember that he had mentioned it.

"You'll not be forgetting that we leave by the Berlin mail to-night," said he. "It's all fixed up that we spend a fortnight in St. Petersburg as the guest of Count Uspensky. I've a wish to see the city, and the arrangement suits me finely. He's a big man there, and has big friends; and he's to have the charge of us. There would be more surprising things than that we should make money there. Ye'll not omit the uniform. It's a poor figure I'd cut in civilian clothes, don't you think?"

I heard him out and then dressed him. You may be sure that I was pleased enough, since Paris was just stagnation then, and it was queer if something did not turn up in a new city and among new people. Little did I think, however, that this was the last journey Sir Nicolas Steele and I were to make together. Yet so it proved, as this story will tell you.

We arrived in St. Petersburg on a Wednesday morning, and by the following Saturday night I had learned enough Russian to bawl "Hisworshik" to a cabman and to get a glass of beer at a bar. The man whose guests we were took us to the Hôtel Klee; but I soon found that we were not to stop long in the city, he being about to set out for the house of one of his kinswomen, whose place was ten miles from Novgorod. And here let me say that Count Fédor Uspensky was never a friend to me, though I stood by him to the end of it. He was a cur right through; a swaggering, bullying, loud-mouthed swashbuckler that set my right arm itching every time he came near me. How it was that he made a friend of Nicolas Steele the Lord only knows. Yet friends they were from the first; and I don't think my master ever did so much for any man as he did for this little Russian captain, who was his host in St. Petersburg. It was a sight to see these two, just as different as chalk from cheese, walking arm- in-arm down the Nevski Prospekt, or ogling the women in Isaac's cathedral. Perhaps it was that each thought he would do the other; perhaps they fell together out of that odd sympathy which men who have known ups and downs show for each other. Any way, they were as thick as thieves; and little it was I saw of them during the five days we spent in the city.

This didn't matter to me, you may be sure. If ever there was a town to let a man play the fine gentleman, that town is St. Petersburg. The very breadth of the streets, the miles of palaces, the over-stocked shops, put a sense of gentility into you. Turn where you will, there are uniforms and pretty women to see. The whole city loves to kowtow to its great folks; even a gentleman's gentleman can find plenty to touch their hats to him and call him excellency. I lived like a fighting-cock the whole time I was there; and when the day came for us to move into the country, there was no man less pleased than I was. Nor did I understand, until Sir Nicolas told me, why we should move at all.

"It's this way," said he, speaking at bedtime on the last night we were at the Hôtel Klée— "there's a cousin of the count's to be married, and we're to go to the wedding with him. Rich people they are, let me tell you, the widow and daughter of Field-marshal Pouzatòv that was. The girl carried on with my friend a couple of years ago, and he's fretting to see the last of her. It wouldn't be decent to stand against this whim. We'll just have a week in the country, and there will be the end of it. Ye'll take plenty of silver with us, for you can't look up to the sky in this cursed place without tossing a rouble to the angels."

He spoke light enough, but his talk would have been different if he had known the black thing we were to see at that very Novgorod, and the end of those three days in the country. He hadn't an inkling of it then, however, and I was no wiser, needless to tell. All I saw before us was a holiday in a Russian village; and while that was not much to look forward to, I remembered that a wedding might smarten things up a bit. "There'll be girls about," said I, "and plenty to eat and drink; and though the women here have got faces like frying-pans, I'll manage to put up with them for a day or two." And with this to keep my spirits up, I packed his bag again, and set off with him to Novgorod by the early morning train.

It was about half a day's journey from the city to Mme. Pouzatòv's place, and when we arrived at the station, there were two four-horse carriages —"chatevkas" they called them-waiting there to meet us. I saw at once, from the silver on the harness and the cut of the horses and men, that we'd come to a slap-up house; and by and by, when the count and Sir Nicolas had done bowing and scraping to the young lady who sat with another gentleman in the first carriage, I came to the conclusion that the people we were to stay with were the right sort. As for miss, she was the best imitation of a pretty girl I had seen in Russia; and though I never had an eye for dark-haired women myself, I could not help but be struck by Marya Pouzatòv. It was as good as a glass of wine any day to see her laugh. She had those speaking black eyes which would make the fortune of the plainest woman alive. And chatter—I believe she talked from the minute we came out of the station until she pulled up the steaming horses at her own door.

I have said that the drive, from the great Moscow railway to the house where the wedding was to be, might be reckoned at an hour. It wasn't a pretty drive, for the country was as flat as a carpet, and what trees I saw were pines in square-cut clumps. We passed a few ragged peasants on the dusty road, and met a priest going to market; but for right down loneliness and desolation send me to the Czar's dominions, and I'll never ask to see any thing worse. I was glad enough when the house came in sight at last—a long white building for all the world like three or four bungalows planked down together. There was an attempt at a bit of garden round about it, and what the people would have called a park beyond that; but it was not until you were inside the house that the means of the lady who kept it were displayed; and that they were first-class I never had a doubt. It was a mansion fit for an English nobleman; and many's the nobleman's place I've been into that wasn't a patch upon it. As for Sir Nicolas, he was beside himself from the start, and when I took him up his hot water for dinner, he could do nothing but talk about it.

"'Tis beautiful quarters we've found, entirely," said he, "and pretty people. I don't suppose ye've much to say about the money here. Faith, I'm beginning to wish I was the general myself. There's twenty thousand goes with the girl, the count tells me, and the reversion of the place. It's many qualities in a wife I could dispense with at a price like that."

"So she's to marry a general, sir?" asked I.

"No one else," said he, "but General Stolitzoff, that was against Osman Pacha before Plevna. A great man, with as many medals on his coat as I have buttons,"

"He wouldn't be young, sir?" I suggested.

"He would be fifty-five, I'm told, and young at that. It was her father's wish on his death-bed that she should have him; but she leads him the devil's own dance, from all I hear. Truth, she's a very sweet little woman-and then there's the money."

"Is the wedding soon, sir?" I asked.

"It's for to-day week, but we'll have a gay time between. They dance to-morrow when the general comes from Novgorod-lucky devil that he is!"

After this, one did not want to be very clever to learn how the land lay with him. I believe he was in love with Marya Pouzatòv from the start; and it's no wonder if he was. A daintier little thing never stepped out of a drawing-room than the girl I saw go in to dinner that night. It was as good as a play to watch him and the count running after her like lap-dogs, now one, now the other dancing attendance on her, and pluming himself that his was the winning hand. Her sweetheart, you must know, was still away at Novgorod, where his regiment was, and the other two did their best to console her. Not that she wanted much of that sort of thing, for a wickeder little flirt never lived, as Sir Nicolas Steele may have found out by this time. But they weren't behindhand in giving her the lead, as the Irishman would say; and the way the three of them went it was a thing to remember.

This, I must tell you, was on the first night of our arrival at Mme. Pouzatòv's house. They had put me in a good room in the servants' quarters, but I was out in the gardens all dinner-time, and little went on that I did not know about. Not that I found my company dull, for the place was chock-full of servants, and though I didn't understand a word of the lingo, I made myself at home like one o'clock. There's a power of language in the squeeze of a pretty woman's hand, and a kiss on a dark staircase is worth a mint of "parlez-vous" any day. I found myself all the better with the "frying-pans" for want of their chatter; and twenty-four hours hadn't passed before I was best man with the lot of them. Nevertheless, my chief business was to keep my eye on Nicky; and all the pretty housemaids in Russia would not have held me from that.

It was this last consideration which led me, on the night after our arrival, to offer my help to the others who were waiting and serving at the grand ball given to the general and the bridegroom that was to be. I had determined that I would see all that was to be seen; and when I had dressed Sir Nicolas, I found it useful to hang about the corridors and the entrance to the ballroom. In this way I had a good view of the old general himself when he arrived about eight o'clock—a fine, noble-looking old fellow, who carried his years like feathers, and had kindness and courage written all over his splendid face. I thought at the time that Miss Marya didn't exactly burst into tears when she saw him; and this I will say now, that she, and she alone, was responsible for all that happened that night, and afterward. She gave him the cold-shoulder from the start of it; she danced three times running with the count, and twice with Sir Nicolas. I don't believe she spoke five words to her intended from the time he arrived until the doors of the dining-room were thrown open for supper. You could see with half an eye that a storm was brewing, and burst it did with a vengeance not ten minutes after midnight had struck.

Up to this time the general had kept his temper like a man. In all that great ballroom, sparkling with lights, and jewels, and wonderful gowns and dazzling uniforms, there was no finer fellow than he. While swaggering Guards in snow-white tunics clustered round him, and Cossacks aired their splendid coats, and little whipper-snappers danced about all sprinkled over with gold and jewels, he was the man of the evening. Upright, a good six feet in his shoes, wearing a dark-green uniform that fitted his figure like a glove, there was always a kindly smile about his eyes, and a manliness in his bearing which did you good to see. Not once in that long evening did he betray himself by look or gesture. Even when the girl he was to marry passed him on another man's arm, and gave him one of her impudent nods, he merely bowed to her and went on smiling. Only when supper-time came did he push himself forward at all-and then it was to offer her his arm that he might take her into the dining-room.

Now, in the scene that followed, whether the girl acted as she did because she disliked the man, or whether it was pure devilry on her part, I have never been able to convince myself. All I can say is that when the general stepped up to Marya and offered her his arm, she turned away from him to the count; and so the two men were face to face almost at the doorway where I stood.

I write that they were face to face, the old man still smiling, the young one hot with anger and with excitement. But it was the count who spoke first, and in French, as all the folks in the ballroom did that night.

"I am sorry, general," said he, bowing with a sneering politeness which made you mad to see, "but mademoiselle is pledged to me for supper."

"Indeed," said the other, "and by what right, monsieur?"

"Oh, that is a question I should not discuss here!"

"Nor I," replied the general, speaking low and bending down toward him. In the same moment I saw the old fellow flick the count on the right cheek with his glove. Five minutes later his carriage was taking him back to Novgorod.

CHAPTER XIX
SIR NICOLAS PLAYS A PART

There is no need for me to tell you all that followed this bitter little scene. It was just as though you had opened the windows of the ballroom and let in the falling snow. While not more than ten people had witnessed the mishap, the story of it was round the house before half an hour had passed. It broke up the ball like a death might have done. I saw Mme. Pouzatòv herself being led up to her bedroom. Her daughter still carried on defiantly with the count, but it was plain that she was scared and half sorry. The others made haste to call their carriages, or formed little groups to discuss the thing with gesture. The servants crept about like mutes at a funeral. We all knew that the night could end but in one way. The men must fight.

It was broad daylight that morning before any of us got to bed. As for myself, I don't believe I took my clothes off. Not that I cared a penny piece whether the general shot the count, or the count shot the general; but there was so much excitement and talk and running here and there, that sleep was far from my eyes. And so it was with my master. I went to his bedroom at eight o'clock, and found him still in his uniform, sitting at his writing-table and drinking coffee. Though he spoke careless enough, you could see that he was shaking to his finger-tips with excitement; and after I'd heard him out, I knew well where he came into it.

"Hildebrand," said he, "I'm to drive to Novgorod in an hour. The count has asked me to act for him."

"Then they are to meet, sir?" said I.

"Was any other course possible?" cried he. "'Tis not with bank-clerks or bishops that we're dealing, but with gentlemen that have gentlemen's means for their quarrels!"

"But the general is his superior officer; the count can't fight with him, sir-at least, that's the talk below."

"Which is nonsense, ye may tell them from me. 'Tis a case where we'll have to get permission from the authorities, and that will not be refused. Sure, the lady is likely to be looking for a husband when the week is gone."

"What about the count in that case, sir?"

He looked at me slyly, as he could sometimes.

"I doubt that she'll marry the count," said he, and that was all.

That was all, but if he thought that I did not read up the rest, he must have taken me for a fool. "Nicky," said I to myself, "you're playing for your own hand. She won't marry the general now, any way. If he shoots the count, you're alone in the field. And there's twenty thousand goes with her, so you might do worse than that."

It was a new idea to me entirely; and I must say that it stuck in my head all that morning, and was still there when he, and the two that had been with him, came home from Novgorod about six in the evening. The day had been a miserable one, wet and cold and chill; the house was quiet as the grave. Not once, the whole morning through, did I see Miss M&rya or her mother. The guests who had remained overnight went away after breakfast. The only conversation was the question whether the count would kill the general, or the general kill the count. And I, who had not cared a snap the day before, found myself as busy thinking about it as the rest of them. For if the count fell-Sir Nicolas would stay in Russia. I would have staked my life upon that. '

My master came home at six o'clock, as I have said; and his first words to me told what he had done.

"I have a case of pistols in my bag," said he, "and I would be glad to know if they're to be trusted. You may amuse yourself for ten minutes knocking the bark off the trees with them."

"Then it's pistols they've chosen, sir?"

"'Tis so, and the old Muscovite conditions-fifteen paces, and a line to come up to. You'll be ready to leave with me at dawn."

"Do you drive far, sir?"

"Four miles to the woods we passed in the carriage on the road here. The count goes with us. Whether he'll return, God only knows. I'm thinking that he won't."

I didn't say so to him, but I knew that if ever the wish was father to the thought, here was the time. Only let the count go down in the morning, and the field was open to him. What would happen if it turned out the other way, I could not think. But I had a suspicion that, even then, Sir Nicolas was the only one who would get any thing by the move; and I wasn't far wrong, as you will learn presently.

The meeting had been fixed for dawn, as you have heard; but the fact was kept close by those who took the lead, and I don't believe that Mme. Pouzatòv or her daughter knew a word about it. As for the count, he had spent the day in the house of the village priest; and I saw nothing of him until dinner was over, and I was out in the park trying the pistols which Sir Nicolas had given to me. At that time the other must have been coming up to our place to see his seconds, for I found him all at once standing beside me and watching my work curiously.

"*Comment, mon ami*," said he, "you have quarrelled with the trees, then?"

"That's it, sir," said I. "Let's hope there won't be more damage done to-morrow morning than there is to-night."

At this he laughed, rather savagely I thought, for he was most bitter to the general all through it, perhaps because he was a devil at heart, perhaps because he really did feel strong about the woman.

"*Sacré nom d'un nom!*" he went on presently, "that would not please me. He has smacked me with his glove. I will return it to him round a bullet. Let me have the pistol in my hand a moment."

He took it up, for I had loaded it, and aimed it at the nearest tree. I could have laughed when he did not even touch the bark.

"Halloa, sir!" said I, "that won't do in the morning. He's a big man, is the general; but he hasn't quite got the girth of that tree."

"The devil take him, no," said he; "but he will die, nevertheless"—and with this he turned on his heel and went swaggering off to the great house like the dirty swashbuckler he was,

"Go on, my man," said I; "but if it isn't your corpse I put in the carriage to-morrow morning, write me down a tenderfoot. He'll shoot you like a dog, and you deserve it too."

I must say that I could see no other end to it. The general was a notorious pistol-shot; this man did not appear able to hit a cow at ten yards. It occurred to me at the time that Nicky knew of this when he egged him on so hard to refuse an apology, as I heard afterward that he did. Be that as it may, I went to bed saying to myself that Count Fédor Uspensky was as good as a dead man; and I got up, half an hour before dawn, precisely of the same opinion.

It was a bitter morning, dark and cold and stormy. The east wind whistled through the pines in a way most dismal to hear. There was a shower of biting sleet just as we started which almost took pieces out of our faces. We all drank cups of steaming coffee and plenty of brandy with that, wrapping ourselves up just like men going out to sing carols. It had been agreed that, we should pick up the count as we drove through the village. Sir Nicolas and I were alone in the four-horse carriage which Mme. Pouzatòv had lent to us, on the understanding that we were driving into Novgorod to smooth down all the trouble. I felt like a man going to a funeral, and I don't think my master was much better,

"Well," said he, when we turned from the park out upon the bare and lonely high-road to Novgorod, "which of them, I wonder, will live to speak of this morning."

"Both, I hope, sir," said I, "Any way, they should do, if the general can't shoot any better than our man."

"'Tis not that at all," replied he, lighting a cigar, and shivering even in his thick coat—"'tis not that at all, but a very bloody business, this same Russian duelling. Ye'll understand that they fire when they please after the word is given, and that if either man takes a step forward toward the centre line, the other man must do the same. Bedad! it might be plain murder, aud nothing less."

"What if they both fire up in the air, sir?" said I.

"'T would be a miracle," cried he; and just then we drove up to the house of the priest, and the count got into the carriage.

He was wrapped up as we were, a heavy military coat covering nearly the whole of his uniform. I could see that he had been priming himself up with drink, and he spoke like a man acting a wild part. Indeed, to hear him you might have thought that there was no such dare-devil in all Europe; while what he said about the general wasn't fit for the ears of a dog. When we were sick of his boasting-and that was soon-he fell to singing snatches of French songs, bawling, "*Nous, nous marierons dimanche*," by which I took it that he really meant seriously by the girl who had brought all the trouble. And I was precious glad at last when the carriage turned from the high-road into the woods, and it was time for us to get out.

CHAPTER XX
THE HONOR OF COUNT FÉDOR

The duel, as I have stated above, was to be fought under conditions common years ago in the Russian army, but rarely heard of to-day outside Muscovy. As the right understanding of these conditions is necessary to my story, I will say a word here about them. For the matter of that, they are simple enough for a child to follow. You place your men fifteen paces apart, and you draw a centre line seven and a half paces from each man. At the word "fire," it is open to either party to shoot or to keep his charge and advance toward the centre line. But when he advances his opponent must advance; so that, given a couple who really meant business, you might find them shooting each other at arm's length. There is nothing in the code to prevent this; nothing but a man's natural sense of right and fair play. It has been done times without number; it will be done again, so long as men leap at each other's throats for a word, or cross swords for a look from a woman's eyes.

I have given this explanation that you may follow me rightly in what I have to say about this particular meeting-the only duel I ever saw fought out, and the only one I want to see. When we arrived on the ground, our other second, who had driven over from Novgorod, was already measuring the fifteen paces. They had driven a stake into the turf to mark the centre line; and, as for the place chosen, it could not have been better. It was just a natural bit of lawn in the midst of the pine thickets; a little clearing so thick set round with woods that an army might have tramped the high-road and have known nothing of what we were doing. The general himself was al- ready there when we arrived, looking spick and span in his tight-fitting uniform, and having a bow and a smile for every one-even for the count. The surgeon, one from the barracks in the town, was busy chattering like a barber, and offering his brandy-flask to all who would like a nip out of it. As for the others-the general's seconds and our own-they were as busy as bees, and a thundering sight more important. You might have thought they were surveying the ground for a new railway, so carefully did they go over it with their tapes and rules; and it was not until a good twenty minutes had passed that one of them cried, "Gentlemen, we are ready," and I knew that the great play was about to begin.

I call it a great play; but, God knows, my heart was in my mouth-then and until the end of it. It's an awful thing to look upon two men, full of life and health and strength, and to think that one of them may lie in his blood, to die where he falls, before another minute has passed away. I can remember to this hour how my hands shook as I took the pistols out of the case and handed them to my master; I can remember what a strange stillness fell upon us all as the men took up their positions in the silence and the darkness of that gloomy morning. Even the doctor ceased his chatter and his jokes, and shut with a snap the case of instruments he had opened so briskly a moment before. It was as though we were already in the presence of death, and that the awe of death had come upon us.

"Gentlemen, are you quite ready?"

My master put the question in French, and hearing it, I glanced quickly at the two who faced each other. The count, I thought, had a look of bitter hate upon his face; the general was still smiling as blandly as a child. I could hear my heart beating like a pump as I watched them and waited for the word, which seemed a year in coming.

"Gentlemen," my master went on presently, "if you are quite ready" —here he paused —"if you are quite ready, then fire." At this word, he stepped back a pace and I saw him bite his lip in his anxiety. One of the pistols sent a thundering report through the woods almost as the word was given; but no man fell. The general had fired deliberately at the sky, and stood now with folded arms to wait the count's pleasure.

Good God! I have lived that moment a hundred times since that day. An unarmed man, waiting for the deliberate aim of a murderer who would have torn him limb from limb if he could! For that was the position-the old man still with that sweet smile upon his face, the young man toying with his pistol and looking like a madman or a devil. So awful was the suspense that I even heard one of the seconds cry, "For God's sake, fire!" And to this cry another of rage and horror was added a minute later, when every man saw that, instead of firing, the count had taken one deliberate step to the centre line, and that the general had imitated him.

"God of heaven!" roared the doctor at this, "is he going to shoot him like a dog, then?"

The words were still upon his lips when the count took another stride forward. I thought for a moment that the seconds would intervene. I believe to this day that they would have done, if Sir Nicolas had not cried out suddenly, "We can do nothing; he is within his right." Once this was said, the old silence fell upon us-upon all but the doctor, who turned his back upon the scene and burst out crying like a woman. And step by step, slowly, deliberately, with all the malice of a devil's heart, the murderer advanced to his work.

They were within two yards of each other at last; yet even then I could not bring myself to think that those about me would stand by and see such a cruel thing. "The count is just torturing the poor old man," I thought; "he will bring him to the centre and then fire up in the air." This opinion was shared by the others, I make sure. Either that, or they were paralyzed-fascinated like a dumb thing is by a tiger. Once they had cried out, not a man spoke. Silently, with faces flushed, their heads bent forward, they watched the meeting as the two came together at last, face to face, almost heart to heart.

"My God! it cannot be; he does not mean it. It's a play-he does not want his life."

I could not keep the words back as the two men met, and stood for one awful minute on the line together. The general's face was still a beautiful thing to see; the count continued to bend forward, holding his pistol at his side. Not a word was spoken on either side, not a gesture made; they stood there like two statues until, suddenly and horribly, the end came. Whether the count really meant to do as he did, whether it was a devilish impulse, I do not know to this day. Be that as it may, the two were standing as I have described them when, all at once, there was a shrill scream—a woman's scream-from the little thicket near by us. One short suppressed exclamation it was; yet enough to cause the general to turn quickly upon his heel; and in the same moment the count raised his pistol and fired. He had pressed the muzzle hard against the other's breast; he shot him like he would have shot a hound. With one awful ringing cry—a cry that sent the birds screaming from the trees, and echoed again and again in the woods-the old man fell his length upon the grass; and smoke and blood poured together from his gaping wound.

That he was stone dead, that he died as he fell, I did not want any doctor to tell me. As the thing went, I don't believe a man of the party moved for more than a minute after that dreadful deed. We were rooted to the ground, held stiff as much with shame as with sorrow. Even the count made no attempt to leave the clearing; he simply stood there with a sneer on his livid face and the smoking pistol swinging in his hand. If Sir Nicolas-who was the first to throw off the spell-had not pulled him away into the wood, he would have held his ground until one of the others had shot him where he stood; as I am sure they would have done if shame had not held their hands. But my master grasped the situation before they had moved from their places, and beckoning me to follow him, he entered the nearest thicket and disappeared from our view. When I found him two minutes later, he was returning to the clearing with a fainting woman in his arms. It was Marya Pouzatòv, who had witnessed the whole scene from the woods.

"For God's sake, look after the count!" said he; "they will cut him in pieces. Get him back to the village, and run all the way. Ye've not a minute to lose, if ye'd save more bloodshed."

With this he ran on, carrying the fainting girl to the doctor, who was still standing beside the dead body of the old soldier. You may imagine that I didn't lose much time in doing as he had told me; and I was out on the road with Count Fédor while you could add up ten. I found him dazed and muttering, and more like a lunatic than a man. "He laughed in my face," was all he could say—"he laughed in my face, and struck me, the dog!"

"That's all very well," said I; and I could have hit him willing, myself. "I hope you're pleased with yourself. If you want to save your dirty life now, keep your mouth shut and come along with me."

"They cannot touch me," said he fiercely, between his teeth. "I was within my right! There is nothing against my honor."

"Your honor be d — —d!" said I, "and you, too, for that matter. Run, you pig of a Russian, run!"

They say we do queer things on the impulse; and I am certain that it was impulse alone which made Sir Nicolas lift a finger to save such a bad one as the count proved himself on that day. Possibly he had other plans at the moment; possibly he didn't see his way clear with two men dead on the field. And what he thought, I thought, too, in my own way. There had been trouble enough for one morning, and no good could follow a second dose of it. The dirty murderer I was running with was in one way our man. It lay upon me to stand by him-until he was clear of the ground, any way. And stand by him I did, never halting a minute the whole three miles back to the village and to the priest's house. When I left him at last, he was splashed from head to foot with mud, and his face was as white as the paper I am writing on.

"You'll not leave me!" cried he, as I left him. "By Heaven, I'll want all the friends I can get this time to-morrow. They'll tear me in pieces-they'll hunt me like a dog — —"

"You should have thought of that before," said I.

"I never meant to shoot him, I swear it!" said he, staggering into the house. "It was the girl's voice that made me-the she-devil that has played with me for five years, and brought me to this at last. Oh, my God! I'm a doomed man."

He went in with this on his lips, and I turned back to meet Sir Nicolas. The bells of the horses in his carriage were already jangling in the village street; and, presently, I saw my master with his Marya, coming along at full gallop. He did not stop even when he caught sight of me, but drove on straight to the great house, where I followed him as fast as my legs would carry me. I found him doing his best to make things look well to Mme. Pouzatòv, and already taking almost a master's place in the house. But he came to me at once when I arrived; and the first name that passed his lips was the name of the count.

"'Tis a paltry murdering villain he is, and nothing else," said he, drawing me aside in the garden; "but we must stand by him, or there'll be bad talk."

"You don't mean to say that you'll keep him in the village there?" cried I.

He looked at me cunningly, and there was the old sly twinkle in his eyes.

"Not exactly that," said he; "not in the village, nor in the town-nor in Russia."

I began to see his drift, and I could have laughed myself. He knew well that dead men are forgiven quickly. But with the count hounded out of the country, the coast would be clear for him.

"You think, then, that he will go, sir?" I asked.

"He will go in half an hour," he answered quietly, "unless he has a fancy for the bullets of the general's men. They will tear him limb from limb, and not lose much time in the employment. You may look for some of them from Novgorod before the sun sets. And that brings me to the point of it. It is yourself that will see him through to Paris. I've ordered the carriage to be at the priest's house in ten minutes from this time. You will hide him in the bottom of it, and drive to Malo, which is a station on the great Moscow railway. Once you have him in the train, lie is safe. But any way, don't return here, for I'd keep what happens from Miss Marya's ears, at all costs."

"Then I'm to go back to our hotel, sir, whatever happens?"

"Whatever happens," said he; "though I have me doubts that ye'll get through with him."

He said no more beyond finding me money for the journey, and we parted without a hand-shake. I have always regretted that, for it was the last time I saw Sir Nicolas Steele. Twenty minutes after I had left him, I was in the chatevka with the count, and we were driving like madmen to Malo. There was no need for him to hide himself in the bottom of the carriage, as my master had wished, for the road was as lonely and as flat as a desert; and I do believe that we did not see a human being until the station came in sight. As for the count, he never spoke a word the whole way, but lay fuddled with drink and half-sleeping on the rugs which

I had spread for him. When I woke him at last, he hardly seemed to know where he was; and he laughed at all my requests that he should keep himself out of sight while he could.

"Hide myself," said he; "and for what? Because I have shot a man who struck me in the face? Bah, I would do the same for him to-morrow, and for his friends too!"

I was not going to trouble myself to argue with him; and truth to tell, there did not appear to be any thing to fear. The platform of the station Mas deserted, save for a pompous-looking man in a gold-braided hat. Outside there were only a couple of old women selling tea, and a bit of a youth skylarking with them. I left my man in perfect confidence while I went to get the tickets; and when I returned to the waiting-room, he was still sitting on the seat where I had left him. It was only when I came quite close to him that I saw how queer his eyes looked, and how stiff his attitude was.

"Halloa!" said I; and as I said it, I noticed that blood was running down his shirt, "what's the matter now?"

But he did not answer me. He was dead, with a dagger through his heart. There was no longer a boy skylarking with the women outside the station.

CHAPTER XXI
I GO TO AMERICA

It was exactly one month after I had left the body of Count Fédor Uspensky in the hands of the local authorities at Malo that I received a letter from Sir Nicolas Steele-the last I ever had from him. I was then in Paris, whither I had gone direct, as he had told me; and I learned there, for the first time, that he was about to marry the daughter of Field-marshal Pouzatòv, and to settle down for good. At the same time he enclosed me a draft for a thousand pounds, and hinted that henceforth we would do well, perhaps, to take different roads through life.

"You have been a good man to me," said he in that letter, "and it goes to my heart to think that this is the end of it all. Whatever comes, I shall never forget the years in which you have been my servant and my friend. But I know your whims, and that such a life as I now propose to lead would not be the life for you. Accept the enclosed draft as a small token of a great gratitude, and be assured that wherever you are, or whatever you may do, my help will be there for you as you need it."

A fortnight after I received this letter, I was on board a ship bound for America. It was not until many months later that I heard the name of the man who struck down Fédor Uspensky. That name I don't intend to disclose; but this I may say, that the boy I saw skylarking outside the station at Malo was a subaltern in General Strolitzoff's regiment. And how did he know that the count would be at Malo, you ask? Why, Sir Nicolas Steele sent a messenger to tell him, of course.

THE END

www.ingramcontent.com/pod-product-compliance
Ingram Content Group UK Ltd.
Pitfield, Milton Keynes, MK11 3LW, UK
UKHW021922190726
13853UKWH00002B/800

9 788027 340385